Sacred Slaying

A Jessamy Ward Mystery

Penelope Cress, Steve Higgs

Contents

Welcome Home

There's no sadder sight than rain-soaked Halloween decorations the day after the night before. Hollow-eyed pumpkins collapsing in on themselves. Bedraggled cloth ghosts and bin liner witches wind-blasted against porch columns and battered fences. The occasional egg-splattered doorway.

The grey, water-logged streets of Kent were a world away from the baroque tree-lined avenues of Paris where Lawrence and I had walked only a few hours earlier.

It had been an interesting weekend that had ended, as promised, with the man I love bending down on one knee and sliding a stunning diamond solitaire on my ring finger.

Of course, I said yes!

It was so romantic. Afterwards, we enjoyed the rest of our Sunday morning, wandering through the quiet streets, soaking in the last few rays of sunshine.

It wasn't to last long.

Around noon, a torrential storm whipped up the English Channel, or La Manche, cancelling all ferries and sending abandoned garden chairs on adventures across neighbours' lawns.

Fortunately, we had booked passage on the Eurostar. No winds can delay an underwater train.

Safely deposited on the right side of the White Cliffs of Dover, we faced the challenge of not drowning under the flimsy convertible roof of Lawrence's sports car. This proved easier said than done. As my fiancé navigated our way back home through sheets of rain, I held tight to the battered inside trim of the canvas that stood between us and the heavens above.

"So, when shall we tell everyone?" Lawrence beamed. Even the weather could not dampen his spirit.

I waved my left hand over the dashboard. "I think they will be so dazzled by this rock we won't need to."

"Well, most of them knew I was going to pop the question anyway, so…"

"Was I the only one out of the loop?" I folded my arms in mock indignation. All those years at drama school were finally being put to good use. Not that Lawrence had time to register my Oscar-winning performance. The raging wind tugged at the corner of the roof above my head, forcing me to end my protest seconds later.

"Don't pretend you didn't know what I had planned."

You're right, we are so empático." Lawrence's knowledge of French had been humbling, so I took every opportunity to throw out any foreign words I knew. I looked at him coyly. "Frederico taught me a few words in Portuguese."

"Oh, did he?"

A plastic carrier bag skimmed its way up the car's windscreen and over the leather top to attack the car behind. *My fingertips are turning blue.*

"That was dangerous. Perhaps we should pull over at a service station or something and sit out the worst of it?" To be honest, regardless of the inclement weather and my numb digits, I wanted to delay our inevitable return to normality for as long as possible.

The fortnight ahead was All-Hallows-Tide, sometimes called All-Saints-Tide, and marks the end of the Church's year. We gear every service around death and remembrance, war and peace, penitence and martyrdom, loss and hope. Peace and hope are fine. Soon it will be Advent and we will look forward to the birth of Christ our King. I do not, however, look forward to mourning those who have passed, and memorials for the wasted youth of the two world wars on Remembrance Sunday are always upsetting.

The season mirrors our vigil. Everywhere is darkness and decay. November nights are endless, whilst the days wither and die within hours. The burnished leaves, so beautiful on the trees, will soon become slippery mulch on the frosty roadsides. The only positive is the lure of cosy nights snuggled in front of a roaring fire.

And now I have a fiancé to nestle up with.

Lawrence motored on. We were losing daylight and still had to catch the ferry to Wesberrey if it was running.

"I am sure Reverend Cattermole will put us up for the night if required." Not as romantic as a suite at Le Roi, where we had spent the past few nights, but any port, or vicarage, in a storm.

Ten minutes later, the rain stopped, the clouds parted and the afternoon sun broke through for a quick game of hide and seek before bedtime.

The motorway stretched before us. Dangerous surface water bubbled on the rolling tarmac, but otherwise, the rest of our journey to Oysterhaven was clear. The Wesberrey ferry though was still a welcome sight as it pulled into the dock as we arrived.

I made casual conversation with Bob, whilst Lawrence parked his car in a garage he rented a short distance up the road.

"Let's have a look then, Vicar." Lawrence was right. Everyone knew, even Bob McGuire. I held out my left hand, which Bob took with admiration. "Bet that cost him a few weeks' salary. Must be something wonderful to have found that special someone, eh?"

I knew Bob still carried a torch for my baby sister, Rosie, but that ship, or rather ferry, had sailed years ago. Technically, Rosie remained married to Teddy until her divorce came through and even then, I think she had already set her eyes on the Texan stallion - Buck.

"It's never too late. Look at me and Lawrence, or Phil and Barbara. You can find someone too."

Bob stared wistfully across the water. "Oh, I have, Vicar. Problem is, she hasn't found me."

Eager to change the subject, I inquired about his sister Mandy and her children. "Did the kids go trick or treatin' yesterday?"

"They did a few houses before it got too dark, bless their hearts. Just as well, though, with that there killer on the loose."

I've only been away for a few days!

"What killer? Who died now?"

"A newbie from the estate. Probably know him to see, but wouldn't be able to point him out in a crowd I don't think." Bob waved across to Lawrence to get him to speed up. "Your fiancé had better get a move on. I only brought her out because I knew you were due back. Another squall is heading to us from around the headland."

"Do the police have a name?"

"PC Taylor said Moorcroft or Moorfield. Do you know him?"

My eyes drifted up to the top of their sockets as if doing that would enable me to see into my memory bank. It didn't work. "No, I don't believe I do. Was he a young man?"

"No. Retired gentleman with a golden retriever. You know, moved into one of those bungalows at the back of the estate that looks out over the western cliffs."

I nodded. "They only just finished building them. Maybe it was an accident. Those cliff paths are dangerous."

"Doubt it. PC Taylor said they did for him with a nail gun. Some Do-It-yourself nut going berserk on Pebble Beach."

Lawrence hopped up the gangway. "Sorry to keep you waiting, Bob. What did I miss?"

As Bob cast off, my phone rang.

It was Aunt Pamela.

Lawrence rested his chin on my shoulder. "Don't answer it. These are our last few moments alone together. Whatever it is, can wait."

I blew him a kiss and hit the decline button, but my heart hung heavy in my chest.

Something was wrong.

I leaned back into Lawrence's muscular arms and closed my eyes.

"Let's get married at Christmas," I said.

My fiancé nuzzled the nape of my neck. "That's in two months' time."

"Yep, I know. I want to set a date before we hit the harbour.

"Won't you be a little busy saying midnight mass and stuff?" Lawrence nibbled my ear.

We were in public, but I didn't care. It's the time of year to create plans for the future. To appreciate the blessing of still being alive.

"Boxing Day then," I replied.

He planted a kiss on the back of my head. "Deal, December 26th, it is."

My coat pocket vibrated. "I'll have to get this, sorry."

It was Pamela, again.

"Hi Aunt Pam, everything okay?"

"Jess, oh thank goddess. Please come quick. The police have arrested Byron!"

Enter DS Stewart

We grabbed one of the waiting horse-drawn taxis on Harbour Parade, and within twenty minutes, luggage flung in the hallway, I was at Pamela's kitchen table. My mother and Aunt Cindy kept vigil. There were no words. Only tearful sniffs punctuated the anxious silence.

You would think it was my uncle who had been murdered!

Lawrence finally broke our sombre scene. He said he was going to brew a fresh pot of tea. Now, clattering around in the kitchen, it sounded more like he was cooking a hog roast, and the pig was still alive.

The noisy interruption offered a chance to move on the conversation.

"So, where is Dave? Surely he can sort this out." I wondered aloud.

Mum had draped her arm around her older sister's shoulder. "They're away. It's been like the Marie Celeste 'round here this weekend. What with you two in Paris and Zuzu and Dave visiting his family."

"Ah, yes, it's half term, isn't it? Makes sense. They can spend more time with his kids. Surely Dave didn't leave PC Taylor alone to handle a murder investigation."

Cindy rubbed the top of Pamela's forearm. "Darling one, they sent over some fresh young thing from New Scotland Yard. A woman. Dave assures me she's an excellent copper and everything should be okay, but she wants a quick win. I'm afraid she'll stop looking for anyone else."

"But I don't understand. Why would they even suspect Uncle Byron in the first place?"

"They found the murder weapon in his beach hut." Pamela wailed. "His stupid hobbies. They set him up, you know."

"Of course, we know Byron wouldn't hurt a fly." Mum patted Pam's shoulder and drew her close. "It's all some terrible mistake."

"Aunt Pamela, who do you mean by 'they'? The police? I heard the murderer killed the victim with a nail gun. Every middle-aged man on Wesberrey owns one. Why pick on Uncle Byron?"

Pamela's soft trickle of tears turned into a torrent. She mumbled something about 'the blasted beach squad' and "she warned him". Getting anything sensible or remotely useful from her was unlikely.

I hoped that Mum or Cindy could fill in the blanks. It seemed flimsy evidence to me. A nail gun, unlike a pistol or revolver, would not leave evidence like gunpowder residue. "Are they sure it wasn't just a tragic home improvement gone wrong?"

"They found him on the beach outside Byron's hut." Cindy sighed.

This was possibly not the best time to say that I didn't even know my uncle had a beach hut. As usual, yet another example of finding out about the family stable after the horse has bolted. "Where's the body now?"

Cindy smiled. "In the hospital morgue. With the storms they haven't been able to transport it to the mainland... yet."

"But if the weather continues to brighten, they will in the morning." Mum pulled away from her sister. "Jess, you need to visit the corpse. See what you can find out."

I could sense my eyebrows arching. "You want me to break in and try to commune with a corpse?"

Mum reached over. "Of course not, dear. Sam will let you in, I'm sure. Why don't you call her? I'll go help Lawrence in the kitchen. Congratulations, by the way, the ring is beautiful."

Thanks for noticing.

"Aunt Pam, I want to help. I really do. But the last two times I ghost whispered, Dave was with me. I can't go tampering with evidence on my own. It will make matters worse."

Cindy looked at her distraught sister and then back at me. "Darling, then wear gloves. They have plenty of them at the hospital. I'm sure Sam will give you some if you ask nicely."

Oh, to be back in Paris.

"Can I use the landline? My mobile still thinks I'm in France."

*****

Sam answered the phone before I even heard it ring on the other end.

"That was quick!"

"Well, I guessed you would be calling. Maybe you're not the only one with a sixth sense." She chuckled down the line. "Get here as soon as you can. I have a hot date tonight."

I walked back to the hospital as quick as my legs could carry me. After three solid days of sightseeing, I wasn't going to break any Olympic records. My ankles screamed their displeasure as I dashed up the slight incline to Upper Road.

Mum promised to explain everything to my fiancé. First night in Wesberrey and they had already separated us. My December wedding couldn't come soon enough.

I didn't even have time to announce the date!

Sam was tapping her feet impatiently at the hospital entrance. "Let's see the rock, then. You need to learn how to take better WhatsApp photos. Lighting, it's all about the lighting."

"Hi Jess, congratulations on your engagement. I'm so happy for you. Lawrence is such a fine man." I mocked in a whiny voice. "All anyone is interested in is this lump of carbon."

Sam pulled off her spectacles and used the lenses as a magnifying glass. "And a stunning lump of carbon it is, too. You have my approval."

We walked down the back stairs toward the basement. "So, your hot date. Is that with Leo Peasbody, or shouldn't I ask?"

"Of course it's with Leo. He came over to take the body to the mainland just before the storm hit. How was Paris?"

"Exciting. I'll tell you all about it later. Let's get this over with as soon as possible." Talking to the recently departed had become a normal part of my life much quicker than I cared to acknowledge. There was a time, not so long ago, when I disbelieved it was even possible. Now, I accepted conversing with the dead as something I had to live with, like the scar on my knee from a childhood game of hop-scotch.

When I was still in primary school, I made an epic leap from square number five to ten. I twisted my ankle on the landing, fell over - navy knickers in the air - and ripped my knee on a raised pavement slab. I hated the mark for years. The silver thread of the wound never tanned and served as a constant reminder of my clumsiness. However, if my headless corpse ever ended up on one of these metal gurneys, at least this injury would help them identify my body. It was part of me now and over time I have grown to accept it.

Gloves snapped on, Sam pulled out the latest of Wesberrey's murder victims. Before us lay the late Greg Moorfield, an elderly newcomer to the island, dressed in a checked red flannel shirt, cream trousers, and blue padded windbreaker. He was unremarkable, except for the fatal nail gun wound between his eyes.

"Should have been quick." Sam prodded the hole gently. "The killer would've had to have got up close and personal to do this. I can't see any signs of a struggle. I think they took poor Mr Moorfield by surprise."

I dragged a chair over to get more comfortable. "Have you met the new inspector?"

"Oh, DS Tippi Stewart. Named after the actress, I believe. The one in The Birds. She's just passed her exams, I think. Looks good in an M&S suit. Reminds me a bit of Dana Scully."

I took Mr Moorfield's hand. "The woman from the X Files."

"Yes. The truth is out there." Sam giggled.

"Well, let's hope Greg here can help us uncover it. Detective Sergeant Stewart has arrested my uncle."

"I know." Sam pulled up a seat opposite me. "They're holding him at the Cat and Fiddle. Guards stationed outside his room, so I've heard."

"Right. Well, let's not waste any more time. Do you have a record button on your phone?"

Sam pulled her mobile from a large pocket in her white lab coat. "Tell me when you're ready."

The Beach Squad

I tried to quiet my thoughts, but the frantic drumming of my heart made it hard to concentrate. The beat pulsed through my body. My ears clogged up like I was underwater. The room spun around me.

"Jess, are you okay?"

Sam's voice seeped in and out of my consciousness. A nauseous lump formed at the back of my throat. I tried to respond, but my words lodged behind whatever was forming in my mouth.

I let go of Mr Moorfield's hand. Everything abated. "I can't do this!"

"Did you talk to him?"

"No. I just felt ill. But he died from a shot to the head. It makes no sense."

Sam leaned across the corpse to comfort me. "Do you want to try again? I'm here to revive you if it all goes pear-shaped."

"That's a comfort." I quipped. I centred myself and took a deep breath. "Okay, I'm going in."

I took Greg Moorfield's hand a second time.

Mr Moorfield. I want to connect with you. I want to find out who did this to you. Can you hear me?

Crickets.

Greg, please. I understand this is all a bit of a shock, but if you can try to talk, I will tell the police what you know.

This was unfamiliar territory. Before I had clear voices or felt a presence. Maybe his soul had already passed over. "I can't reach him. I think I'm too late."

"Jess, this is for your uncle. You can't give up."

"Don't you think I know that, Dr Hawthorne?" I snapped. "Sam, I'm sorry. Perhaps I'm too emotionally invested."

"Maybe you are." Sam pushed back her chair and walked towards the door. "Or maybe you are simply dehydrated. Have you had anything to eat or drink since leaving France?"

I shook my head. I never got to sample that tea Lawrence was making.

"Right, well, I am prescribing some liquid refreshment. We can come back in half an hour."

"But what about your hot date?"

"Oh, Leo likes the anticipation. He can simmer on the pot until I am ready." She sniggered.

The image of Leo Peasbody getting hot under the collar was hard to imagine, but then I only knew him in his professional capacity. Not a lot of call for fiery passions in the funeral business.

*****

21

Hot tea with a dash of Scotch whiskey warmed my autumnal heart. Duly fortified, we returned to the morgue. Mr Moorfield lay as before. Not that I was expecting him to have moved.

Restored, I took his hand again for the third time and closed my eyes.

Mr Greg Moorfield. This is Reverend Jessamy Ward, your parish priest. I know it's hard to understand but I can also talk with the recently deceased. Sorry to say that is what you are. Someone murdered you, Mr Moorfield, and the police have arrested my uncle, Byron. Can you help tell me who really did this to you?

There was a shuffling sound to my right.

Sam heard it too. "Jess, open your eyes."

"What? I'm busy."

"I really think you'll want to see this."

I blinked my way back into the room.

Sam was pointing to my right side.

The next few moments were in slow motion. I shrugged my shoulders, then twisted my head to the right. Mr Greg Moorfield was standing next to me. Well, at least, a pale, wispy version of him was.

"Sam, you see him too?"

"Uh-huh."

"What was in that tea?"

"Nothing. Ask him some questions then." She muttered. I didn't need to look to know the last phrase was through clenched teeth.

"Mr Moorfield. Er, thank you for joining us. Can I ask you a few questions, please?"

He nodded. *Maybe he can't talk?*

"Great. Right, er, do you know who killed you?"

Mr Moorfield nodded sadly.

I have to ask...

"Was it my Uncle Byron?"

There was a pause. Greg closed his eyes and eventually shook his head.

Sam clapped behind me, and then immediately apologised. "So sorry, but that's great news."

"Yes, but I don't know who else to suggest. Mr Moorfield, can you tell me or maybe show me who did this to you?"

A mist formed over his sad eyes. He drew a zip over his shadowy mouth.

"You can try to talk to me in my head. I can usually hear people."

Greg glanced to the side. A white glow filled the room.

It's now or never.

"Mr Moorfield. Was it a member of the beach squad?"

He turned and disappeared into the light.

"Sh-should I take that as a yes?" I stuttered.

"Oh my word, in all my years of medical practice, I have never encountered anything like that before."

"Well, you said you had a sixth sense."

"I was joking, obvs."

"Obvs? What are you, fourteen?"

"In need of another cup of special tea, is what I am." Sam re-covered the body with a white cloth. "Who are the beach squad?"

"I don't know. Just something Pamela said earlier. I didn't know what else to ask?" I possibly had missed my opportunity to find the solution. "But I'll take a rain check on that special tea. I need to get to see my uncle before they take him away."

*****

Walking back to the vicarage to fetch my scooter, I chastised myself for not getting more information from the late Mr Moorfield. Only this morning I was the happiest love-struck lady vicar on the planet, now I was a slightly tipsy, though still legal, psychic priest on a mission to save my uncle. My stomach grumbled as I mounted Cilla for a late evening ride into town. I paused only to update the 'Charmed' sisterhood and my fiancé by phone. There was no time to lose. Detective Sergeant Stewart would take my uncle away on the first ferry in the morning unless the weather worsened overnight.

I thought about walking into the public saloon and nonchalantly walking up the main stairs to the bedrooms, but it was dinner time and there was an excellent possibility that DS Stewart and her team were tucking into some of Phil's pub favourites. The back stairs through the kitchen seemed the best bet.

I crept past the meal preparation area like a ninja. Barbara's voice carried through from the bar. She was talking to Phil, so I knew where they were. I really didn't want to have another discussion about my engagement ring right now.

Successfully to the foot of the back stairs, I realised I didn't know which room Byron was held in. I would start at the top and work my way down. There were only three floors.

I determined that the best approach was to stride with purpose along each corridor. The room was guarded, which meant uniformed police officers stood outside. It would be easy to spot.

I should have started on the first floor.

"Hello, officers, I'm Reverend Jessamy Ward, Vicar of St. Bridget's." I puffed.

I had to persuade the police guards stationed outside his make-shift cell that I was only there to offer religious comfort to a member of my flock.

"I believe you are holding one of my parishioners on a charge of suspected murder? He's quite an elderly gentleman, easily confused. This must be terrifying for him. He also has a heart murmur, I believe." The two constables looked at me blankly. "I was wondering if I could offer him some solace at this difficult time."

They each turned to check permission from the other, then the closest to the handle opened the door.

That was too easy.

I knocked, and a familiar voice called to come in.

I smiled at the officers before slipping into the room. "Shh, Uncle Byron, it's me." I placed my finger against my lips.

The key turned in the lock behind me.

"Wow, they are being ultra-secure."

Byron was sitting on the end of the bed, watching a gardening programme on BBC2.

I had rarely spoken to my uncle. In company, at least, my aunt was the most vocal. They were an interesting coupling. She, an understated believer in the Goddess whose beige attire hid the fact she had a spare room devoted to spells and potions. And he, a grey shadow figure who spent most of his time with his model railway or down the garden centre.

I wedged my rear beside him to watch the television. "Ah, Monty Don. He's a national treasure."

"Oh, yes, Jessamy. Pammie prefers that awful Alan Titchmarsh. She's even bought some of his terrible books. I doubt it's his real hair."

I looked at Monty Don's Sideshow Bob mop of loose curls and doubted anyone would buy a wig like that. "Looks real to me."

"Not Monty Don's, that Titchmarsh fellow." he huffed.

"Uncle Byron, do you know why they have arrested you?"

He stared at me for a full ten seconds. I imagined in complete disbelief I could be asking him something so inane.

"That fool Moorfield got himself killed over a piece of whale vomit."

My expression was probably as blank as my mind.

"Oh, Jessamy." He sighed, "I had you down as the bright one. Ambergris?"

I now had images of my usually verbally challenged uncle disappearing into his shed to assign scores to some secret league table where he assessed my sisters and me on brains, beauty, and wit.

Jess, ask the obvious question!

"I'm sorry. What is ambergris?"

"I've told you already. You really should pay more attention."

I think I prefer the Uncle Byron who doesn't speak.

"You only mentioned whale vomit."

"Yup, ambergris." Byron leaned backwards to retrieve the remote control. "They should be here with my dinner soon. So listen up." He pressed the mute button and turned to face me square on. "Moorfield joined the Beach Squad a few months ago. He wanted to meet people. He'd retired here from the mainland, you see, and didn't know a soul. Anyway, we had only been out a couple of times. Beaches get too crowded in the summer for any decent finds. Too many tourists."

I needed him to wind back a little.

"Uncle, before you go any further. What is this Beach Squad?"

"Just a few old-timers like me. We scour the beach at low tide looking for treasure. Well, the others do. I am more interested in our feathered friends. I'm an amateur ornithologist."

"I didn't know you were a twitcher. You're a man of many hobbies."

"Anything to get out of the house when Pammie's sisters are over. All their cackling makes my head hurt."

"Okay, so you are bird watching. And the rest?" I asked.

"Ah, yes, well. There's Kenneth, Kenneth Wilson. He's a retired accountant. Did a bit of National Service back in the day, though from what I hear, he spent more time in the glasshouse than anywhere."

My ignorance this evening appears to know no bounds.

"The glasshouse?"

"Jail. He was a bit of a spiv, by all accounts. Always looking to reap some financial benefit."

Mental note: look up 'spiv' when I get home.

"And is he a bird watcher too?"

Byron laughed so hard he dropped the remote. "No! Good old Ken is a metal detectorist, looking for Roman coins and stuff."

"So why would he be interested in whale vomit?" The more Byron spoke, the more confused I became.

"To sell it, of course. Just like all the rest of them. It's worth a fortune."

Second note to self: look up ambergris.

"Okay," I pretended the proverbial penny had dropped. "And who are the other members of the Beach Squad, then?"

"Well, that would be Captain Roger Cummings, served with the Queen's Own Buffs, The Royal Kent Regiment, in the early sixties. Saw action all over the world. Kenya, Borneo, Hong Kong. Decent chap, a little rigid."

"So they are both military types. Is Captain Cummings a detectorist as well?"

"Hardly. He's our local litter champion. Not just the beaches. He walks miles every day, picking up the rubbish the rest of us so casually toss aside. You must have seen him around. The man deserves a medal."

I wish I had brought a notebook.

"Anyone else?"

"Yup, just one more regular. Paul Meacham. Shaggy-haired chap looks for driftwood, shells and the like. Sells them on eBay. Looks a bit like that comedian. Scottish fella."

"Billy Connolly?"

"That's him. Paul hails from London originally. Grammar schoolboy done good. Has lived here for years."

"Right, well, that's quite the list of subjects. But, uncle, it was your nail gun. How do you explain that?"

"I'd left it in the hut. We all have access. It's like our secret den, I suppose. We meet there once a week usually, sometimes more. We all appreciate the quiet, you see."

"And you think it's all about this ambergris."

"Don't think. I know. What else could it be? We're just a bunch of old men escaping the real world, none of us have anything worth killing us over. Just don't know which one of them did it."

She's Behind You

The opportunity to ask more questions dissipated with a firm knock on the door. Byron, eager to make the most of his enforced vacation, told the owner of the firm knock to come right in.

It was Tilly. "Oh, good evening, Reverend. I would have brought up two dinners if I knew you were here. If you want, I can run down and get you something."

"No need for that, young lady. Reverend Ward was just about to leave."

Was I?

Byron winked.

"Y-Y-Yes, I was. I'll come down with you."

I thanked the officers for their kindness as they locked Byron back in his room to enjoy his three-course meal.

A voice called down the hall. "Excuse me, Reverend. Might I have a word?"

I slipped a glance at Tilly, who bobbed like a servant in *Above Stairs* to someone behind me and made quick her exit.

DS Stewart.

Serviceable heels pounded the wooden floorboards.

I pivoted on mine.

"Ah, Detective Sergeant Stewart, I presume. I heard you are heading up this case. If I can be of help in any way, please don't hesitate to ask."

"You can help me by staying away. PC Taylor was kind enough to bring me up to speed on your amateur sleuthing ways. I also understand that my primary suspect is your uncle."

I could see what Sam meant by the new police investigator having an air of Gillian Anderson, though right now she reminded me more of her portrayal as Prime Minister Margaret Thatcher in *The Crown*, if Maggie had sported a short grey-blonde wedge-cut and wore a trouser suit. "I was visiting Byron as he's a member of my parish and, of course, family. I'm sure you understand."

DS Stewart took two bold strides towards me. "Oh, I understand. I also *understand* that DI Lovington is romantically involved with your sister. Quite the family affair here, isn't it?"

"Well, yes. It's a very, er, close-knit community. Anyway, this is your case, and I'm sure you will investigate all angles before making any rash decisions."

The detective sergeant folded her arms across her chest. "Are you questioning my decision making so far?"

"Well, what about the nail gun? How do you know that's my uncle's?"

She raised her right hand and assumed a melodramatic thinking pose.

"Oh, I don't know. Could it have been his name written on the bottom of the gun with a black Sharpie?"

I have no answer to that.

"Don't worry, Reverend Ward, I will ensure it's sent to the lab for tests. But I have to warn you, my guys dusted for prints and only found one set. So I would say there's a high probability they belong to your uncle."

The truth is out there...

"What's his motive, then?"

"Oh, who knows? A tragic senior moment, perhaps. An argument over a chess move. What do old men fall out about?" she sneered. "I will find out. Now, if your business here is complete, may I ask you to vacate the premises?"

"My pleasure."

Ooh, I don't like her. I don't like her at all.

*****

Tilly was waiting for me at the bottom of the stairs.

"I'd like to help you solve this one." Tilly tugged at her shirt cuff. "Mr Moorfield was our next-door neighbour. Dad is devastated. He was very fond of the old man. Used to help him out with chores and stuff. When he called me earlier, he could hear Alfie howling in the kitchen. Poor dog. He must have been alone all night."

"How awful. Has Buck called the vet?"

"Nah, we have a key. Mr Moorfield had no proper family to speak of. Not in the UK. His son, and daughter-in-law, live in Australia. They're not going to fly over to rescue a portly Golden Retriever."

"No, I guess not. So what's going to happen to him?"

"Oh, Dad's a sucker for waifs and strays. Alfie will live with us. Luke is looking forward to taking him on walks with me. Kinda romantic, eh?"

"I guess. I'm not sure I can do any more here. Detective Sergeant Stewart has made it very clear I shouldn't get involved."

"Nonsense. You've never let that bother you before." A coy smile tickled the corner of her young lips. "I'll help you make suspect files, like last time, and bring Alfie down to meet Hugo. I think they'll get on like a house on fire."

Tilly swung from the top of the newel post like an excitable child. It was sometimes hard to remember that her life had not always lent itself to such innocent pleasures.

"I'm not sure Hugo is the sociable type, but otherwise, that sounds like a great idea. It's All Souls tomorrow, so I have to say mass at ten. Do you want to come over for lunch?"

Tilly planted a soppy big kiss on my cheek. "Wild horses wouldn't keep me away. I have to get back to work now. Phil looks all cute and cuddly, but he really cracks the whip. Congratulations, by the way." She smiled and ran off behind the bar.

*****

I called Pamela from my mobile before heading home, reassured her that Uncle Byron was doing fine and not to worry. I was worried, though. There had to be a way to talk to the other members of the Beach Squad without drawing suspicion from DS Stewart.

The heavens opened as I pulled into the final yards of Upper Road. I put Cilla to bed in the garage and dragged my waterlogged, starving body over the vicarage threshold. I was so tired I didn't notice that the door was unlocked, or that the lights were on in the hall and kitchen.

I remained oblivious to everything around me until Hugo weaved himself around my feet.

"Hello, my favourite boy." I picked him up and carried him through to the kitchen on my shoulder.

"Should I be jealous?" Lawrence was pouring out choco-laty goodness from my milk pan into a waiting mug.

Adding up the clues, there was only one conclusion. "Mum lent you her keys, right?"

"Well, I am your fiancé. Here. Sit down. I've made you some cocoa and there's a vegetable tart and some potato salad in the fridge if you're hungry."

"I'm ravenous."

Lawrence plated up.

"Should I expect this level of service every night when we're married?"

Lawrence grinned over his frothy mug. "I won't need to impress you then."

"I'm sorry my family hijacked our engagement. This morning was so romantic. I'm going to miss waking up and seeing your face over breakfast."

Lawrence had been the perfect gentleman whilst we were away. He had arranged for an enormous suite so that we could maintain our agreement to stay chaste until our wedding, alternating between bed and sofa bed each night. He would have slept gallantly on the sofa bed throughout our visit, but his feet dangled over the edge, so I insisted we swap.

"Do you still have your luggage with you?"

He nodded.

"Well, you have a choice of rooms. Only me and Hugo are here now."

Shifting his gaze to scrutinise the cartoon decal on the porcelain container in his hands, he mumbled, "My bag's already upstairs."

*****

Lawrence had been busy. He'd laid out my pyjamas on my bed, and put my toiletries back in the bathroom. His toothbrush snuggled next to mine in the cup. There was a fresh glass of water on the bedside cabinet and an artificial rose placed on my pillow.

We met on the landing for a sweet kiss goodnight.

"Where did you get the rose?"

"I might have borrowed it from the display in your aunt's hall."

"Well, I don't condone stealing, of course, but thank you."

One warm embrace later, I sat tucked up in bed with a sea of romantic dreams swimming around my heart.

Notes to self, remember?

I had put my phone on to charge. *I need to buy a longer cable.* The USB connection was precarious and the taut wire could fall out at any moment, crashing my screen into the dreaded dark abyss of ultimate low battery.

After several attempts to spell ambergris, I pulled up news reports of people finding smelly rocks of whale vomit on beaches across the British Isles, some selling to perfume companies and dealers for £50,000 upwards. Now that kind of find provides a potential motive for murder.

The other word of the day was 'spiv'. Seems it is British slang for a petty criminal, particularly one able to acquire goods from the backs of lorries and sell them on at bargain prices.

Kenneth Wilson had just become my primary suspect.

Burnt Offerings

My turn in the kitchen the next morning offered my future husband an appetising selection of watery scrambled eggs, burnt toast and half-cooked vegan sausages. But my coffee was on point.

Lawrence scraped olive oil spread across his charcoaled bread. "I can see why your mother thinks you should get a housekeeper."

"Cheeky, I usually have a bowl of muesli. This is a rare feast."

He fished yellow lumps of egg from their mini lake. "Hmm, is that a promise or a threat?"

"Well, that's rich, coming from a middle-aged man who's still living with his mother. Do you even know how to boil an egg?" *Attack is the best form of defence.*

"Ouch. Your mother also warned me about your sharp tongue." Lawrence gulped down the remaining bites on his plate. "Anyway, let's think about that housekeeper. We can afford it, and we help support another family who needs the work. Sounds like a win-win to me. Especially if we want to eat anything other than muesli and microwaved meals."

He packed up his adult satchel and kissed me goodbye. I watched him walk down the hall and out through the front door. I crunched a satisfying bite of burnt toast between my teeth.

I could get used to this.

*****

The mass for All Souls, as usual, was a sombre affair. Yet again, the cloud of death hung over the island. From the pulpit, I reminded my congregation that God loves us and, through his grace, we will gain eternal life. Death is merely a portal into the next world.

I hoped to see the promise of salvation on their faces. Part of me wanted to tell them I know there is an afterlife. I have communed with the hereafter and those who have gone before. But the irony is that the doctrine of the church is to believe without proof. The basis of faith is to trust in the universal GPS system. To never question that we will reach our destination if we follow the path laid out before us. To say I can talk to the dead would probably see my licence revoked, and I really dig this uniform.

Few stayed for the coffee morning afterwards. There was an awkward atmosphere. Wesberrey is a small community. Many here would have known Byron for years. Still, the muttering in corners would end abruptly as I drew near. While they held out their hands to offer their condolences, their eyes said, 'There's no smoke without fire.'

Even Phil and Barbara seemed in a hurry to leave.

"I'll be back later to check out the boiler. Getting chilly now. Need to check the old dear is fighting fit for the winter." Phil bundled his wife into a purple anorak with a faux fur-lined hood.

Barbara, unusually, had little to say. Though she stopped to deploy an almighty bear hug before leaving to oversee the pub's lunch menu.

I knew she would be back working in my office in the afternoon, but I saw much less of her now she had married her dream man. They both were so busy, it constantly amazed me how many roles they played in our little community. And always with a ready smile.

Still, I felt they were distant, or perhaps I was being paranoid. It had been a whirlwind couple of days, and I was probably reading too much into things.

Two people noticeably absent from the church were Tom and Ernest. Both had resigned as churchwardens at the end of last month following the start of Ernest's chemo treatment. Ernest first and then Tom when he realised how invasive the treatment would be. I popped over to their house at least once a week. Ernest was doing well, all things considered. Tom, on the other hand, was run ragged.

I had a baptism later, which is always a joy, and then I would go over to the White House and visit my friends. But first, time for lunch.

***

Fortunately for Tilly and Luke, their expectations of my culinary prowess were already low. So low that leftover tart, half a bowl of potato salad and some hastily thrown together vegan cheese and tomato sandwiches almost impressed them.

True to her word, Tilly brought over some cardboard folders, a small corkboard and the gorgeous fluff ball, Alfie.

The plan was for him to play with Hugo, but my cat had other ideas and shot out of the flap in the back door like a bat at twilight. Alfie, unfazed, sniffed around for a bit and then curled up on the rug.

"I thought we could create our own suspect board like they do in the cop shows. I've brought pins and coloured wool. Luke is great with a camera. He'll get some photos. When shall we begin our surveillance?"

"Tilly, I admire your enthusiasm, but I can't sanction the two of you trailing potential murder suspects around Wesberrey."

Luke stuffed the last corner of shortbread pastry in his mouth. "Hold on, need some water."

Water drunk, he continued. "Uncle Byron is my family, too. How else would I know about the wonders of the N gauge over the limitations of OO tracks?"

Tilly giggled. "And not a single day goes by when you don't refer to that knowledge. It's been life-changing."

Luke hit her playfully. "You know what I mean. When we first arrived, he looked after me, you know. I want to help him now. If I can."

"Hmm." I got up to grab myself another cup of coffee. I waved my mug over the corkboard on the table. "And my sister is fine with all this?"

"Yup." Tilly interrupted. "Rosie and Dad discussed it last night when I told them you had invited me to help you. Dad is super keen to get involved too. Whatever you need, just ask."

Buck has keys to Greg Moorfield's house.

"Thank you. I'll bear that in mind. Right then, let's set this up somewhere private. We don't want that new DS stumbling upon it till we are ready, do we?"

We set up a makeshift incident room in Rosie's old room. Lawrence had slept in Zuzu's and Mum occasionally stayed over in her old room, so here there was less chance of our work being disturbed or discovered.

The youngsters soon transformed this tiny space into a cosy den. Luke hung the corkboard. Tilly arranged the folders in an old wire magazine rack, alphabetically, and I caught them both up to speed on everything I knew. Well, everything apart from deciphering the silent gestures of Greg Moorfield's ghost.

"Do we know where the police are storing the evidence?" Luke asked.

"Given that I think the sum total of their evidence is the nail gun, I imagine it's in an evidence bag in Detective Sergeant Stewart's room, until she can get it to forensics."

Tilly sat cross-legged on the floor. "Do you think she knows about the, what did you call it, amber grease?"

"*Amber-gri*, you don't pronounce the S. French for a smelly rock, from what I've read."

"And it's really made from whale vomit. That's so cool." Luke got busy looking up all he could find about ambergris on his mobile.

"To go back to your question, Tilly. No. I don't think DS Stewart has a clue about the whale rock. We need to find where it is now. Whoever has the ambergris killed Greg Moorfield."

Role Reversal

I told my fellow investigators all I could remember about our suspects so that Tilly could make the folders and left them to continue setting up our incident room. I made a hasty beeline for the vestry to change for the baptism.

It was crazy to think that the gurgling bundle wrapped in white satin and lace in my arms, was but a twinkle in his father's eye when I first arrived back on Wesberrey. Welcoming a new brother or sister in Christ to the fold always gladdens my heart. The symbolism of light and cleansing water. The loving declarations of the godparents to provide moral and spiritual guidance to this fragile human being, throughout their time here on earth, is my favourite moment of the ceremony. Families and closest friends stand joined in hopeful prayers for the future that lies ahead. *Is there a better way to spend a dreary, weather-beaten afternoon?*

I think not.

The next task on my to-do list would not be as fortifying. Over my years of service to the Church, I have visited many people diagnosed with the big C, but it is different when they are friends and colleagues. God will decide if Ernest pulls through this battle. I had faith in his divine wisdom.

It was my duty to offer a reassuring word, and the offer of practical support and care, as much for his partner, Tom, as for Ernest himself.

Tom, so far though, had refused all help. The parish community tried to rally around him. Rosemary offered to cook, Barbara to clean, and Phil to help with the garden and do odd jobs, but Tom remained adamant he could cope, thanking us all the same.

He would let me visit under sufferance. The conditions for entry were that I come armed with the latest gossip and stay away from the pastoral stuff. No asking questions about how anyone was coping or what the doctors had to say. He, at least, would want to hear all about Lawrence's proposal in every juicy detail.

Taking a beat to polish up my diamond and position my hand in such a way as to bounce as much of the afternoon sun off the ring as possible, I knocked on their door.

I held the pose for several minutes. *My arm's getting heavy!*

An ominous grey cloud edged ever closer to the sun, and soon the effect would be lost.

I knocked again. Still no answer.

Nursing a stiff shoulder and a disappointed heart - *will anyone ever ask me how he proposed?* I strolled along to the Cliffview station.

Lo-and-behold, there, snuggled inside the station cabin, Tom sat warming his hands on a thermos flask.

"Hello, Tom. I was just at the house. I didn't expect you to be here."

"Today's volunteers let us down. We can't have the old girl out of service, now can we, Reverend?"

"Is Ernest down by the harbour then?"

"Yes. Phil promised to keep him supplied with hot beverages, and Bob McGuire said he would watch him like a hawk."

"Ah, I see. He's not so isolated down there, though arguably colder."

Tom shivered under his tartan blanket. "I think it will do him the world of good. The doctor says he should get out and about as much as possible. Get some vitamin D and fresh air. It's only for a couple of hours. The cavalry is on its way.""I know the island is very grateful for all the volunteers that keep this train going."

"Time to recruit some fresh blood, I think. How times change, eh? When you first arrived, it was just Ernest and me, most days. Summer, we always get some youngsters willing to earn a few pounds, but we need a long-term solution."

"I think we should apply to the council, or even the Lottery Fund, for money to staff it properly. It's a vital service and with all the new buildings going up, we have a strong case."

"Ernest would love that. But don't tell him. You know what he's like. He would want to handle all the legal side and he isn't up to that level of stress."

I rubbed Tom's arm to show that I understood totally. "As I have you alone. I wanted to ask... how are you coping?"

Tom bit his lip and turned his head towards the cliff edge. "You promised not to get all cosy feely with me. I can't think about myself right now. Ernest needs me to be strong. He's always been my rock. I can't bear the thought..."

"You can't look after him if you don't take care of yourself. Remember what they say on planes about putting the oxygen mask on yourself before you help others."

Tom breathed out a heavy, long sigh. "Are you heading down, Reverend?" He rang the string bell to call up the carriage from the station below.

"Tom. I came to see you, but I will pop down and see Ernest, too. I wanted to show you my ring and tell you about Paris."

"That's nice. Glad you had a lovely time."

The huge steel chains ground into action. Moments later, the familiar burgundy and gold livery pulled into view. When locked in place, Tom prised open the metal doors.

"We'll have left when you come back up, I should think. Have a pleasant afternoon, Reverend."

I stepped across the moving gap. The carriage bumped against the platform in the wind. The entire structure creaked. "I'll get onto the council as soon as I can. She just needs some tender loving care, and this old lady will be good for another hundred years."

Tom shrugged and closed the door. Usually, there was a cheery farewell, but today he ratcheted the lever and sent me down without a word.

I am worried about him. Very worried indeed.

***

Ernest, by comparison, was on top form. He greeted me with a ready smile and a wave.

"Reverend! I hear you have some good news for us. Did it all go according to plan?"

Finally, someone was interested in hearing about my engagement.

"Not exactly," I smirked, "but it was still unbelievably romantic and a truly memorable trip."

"I imagine Tom was all over your ring. Lawrence did hint he had one in mind, from a Parisian jeweller. Do you mind if I take a look?"

Have Tom and Ernest traded personalities?

"Of course not." I dangled my ring finger under Ernest's nose. He calmly took my hand and held it up towards the light to get a clearer view.

"I'm no connoisseur, but that looks impressive. Have you set a date?"

"We have, but I've told no one yet."

"Not even Tom? How did you get past him without offering up that little secret?"

I wanted to say because he's too worried about you to think about anything or anyone else. I wanted to hug them both so tight all the hurt would run off with the wind. Instead, I smiled and lied. Sometimes it is the right thing to do. "Oh, he tried to get me to squeal. I'm just wise to his ways."

"Well, Reverend, teach me your tricks. I fall for his charms every time."

Ernest's mask cracked just enough to let out a single tear. I knew better than to draw attention to it.

"Tom said you wouldn't be on duty for long, so I'll probably miss you on the ride back."

"Yes, just emergency cover. It's been rather enjoyable, a trifle brisk. The air, that is, not business. The tourists have gone. Well, it is November now."

"Indeed. The months have flown by."

"So, Reverend, I guess you are off to prove your uncle is innocent of all charges. Just to let you and your aunt know, no one believes it was Byron. There's not a bad bone in that man's body."

"Well, the police don't appear to be looking at any other suspects. Byron mentioned the Beach Squad. Do you know who they are?"

"Of course, all of us old men know each other," he laughed. "A motley bunch of people with too much time on their hands. They could fill their hours with useful service to the community, instead they roam the beaches looking for treasure."

"Doesn't one of them collect litter?"

"Roger, yes. Oh, trust me, he has plenty to say about the others when they are not around."

This is bizarre. Gossip is usually Tom's territory.

"Roger Cummings is ex-military, right? I imagine that makes him a stickler for rules."

The bell rang. Someone else must be waiting for the train above us. Ernest closed the door and yanked the lever.

"I suggest you pay him a visit. He lives on the other side of Market Square. You know the house. Has a huge Union Jack on a mast in the front garden. Very neat privet hedge and some fine rose bushes, though I doubt there are any petals left after that storm. There's not a leaf left on the boughs in our garden. A nice little job for when the wind drops."

"We can get someone in to rake the lawn for you. I'm sure Luke won't mind."

"Thank you, but I'm not dead yet."

Game On

I arrived at the ferry terminus just in time to see DS Stewart march my uncle on board. His hands were pulled behind him in handcuffs.

I called out above the engine noise, but neither of them heard me over the diesel motors.

I watched the ferry pull away from the dock. Byron sat slumped between the detective sergeant and a uniformed officer. There would be no satellite television in Stourchester jail, and the food would not be up to the standards of the Cat and Fiddle.

I closed my eyes and said a prayer for his safe return to us, and threw in a couple of words for Tom and Ernest, too. It was all I could do. I had to believe it had some effect.

The ferry gone, Harbour Parade fell silent. There was no market today, and the bitter winds had driven most of the locals to stay indoors. Only a few determined cats crawled along the front, hunting for any remaining morsels of the morning's catch.

I crossed the desolate square, the trailing gusts of yesterday's squall picking up abandoned food wrappers and leaves like tumbleweed. Rosie, suitably wrapped against the elements, was outside Dungeons and Vegans wiping down the cast iron tables and chairs.

"The *Charmed* are inside if you're looking for them."

I wasn't, but now I know where my mother and her sisters are, I have to pop in.

"Rosie, thanks. Erm, Luke and Tilly are up at the vicarage. They said you were okay with them helping me. I just wanted to check —"

"Yeah, that's fine. I was thinking perhaps Buck and I could join you for dinner later, pool ideas. He's been asking around. Looking for witnesses. Naturally, he's very keen to find the murderer."

"Yes, of course. The victim was his elderly neighbour. Very sad. I met Alfie earlier. The poor mutt must be very confused."

Apart from Buck and the Beach Squad, it seemed that Mr Moorfield hardly knew anyone on the island. At least that narrowed down the suspect pool.

"So, the sisterhood, where are they?"

"In the gaming zone. It's always quiet back there on a Monday. I will close up soon and join you. Pumpkin Latte?"

"Little Sis, you read my mind."

***

I found the three sisters huddled on a deep, black leather sofa. A pink neon sign screaming 'Game On' flashed intermittently above their heads.

"Hi Aunt Pam, I saw DS Stewart take Uncle Byron on the ferry. He looked to be bearing up okay."

"Just as well, as you haven't found the real killer yet. Why aren't you out there hunting down suspects?" Pam's face fell into a large cotton handkerchief. Mum stroked some hair away from her sister's tear-soaked cheeks.

Cindy unstuck herself from the tacky leather cushions and perched on the edge of the sofa, her elbows resting on her thighs. "Jess, darling, what have you found out so far? Did you speak to Mr Moorfield's spirit?"

I flipped around a chair to face the sofa. "I tried. For some reason, he couldn't or wouldn't speak. He did mime to me that Byron is innocent."

Pam sobbed from behind her broderie anglaise wall. "So nothing, you have nothing. Cindy, I told you we should do this ourselves."

"Aunt Pamela, I assure you I am working on it. I spoke to Byron last night. He was fine, and he gave me some hot leads. I was on my way to meet one of them now."

"Then what are you doing here? I have plenty of caretakers." Pam waved her damp white flag at her sisters. "Just sort this out, Jess. Please."

"After she's drunk her coffee." Rosie plonked down two mugs on the black ash table. "A girl can't sleuth without caffeine in her bloodstream."

The spirals of milky steam scrolled through the air and wrapped themselves around us. Pam's sobbing subsided. A faint drip, drip, drip replaced the sound of her tears.

Mum looked around the basement. "Rosie, do you have a leak?"

My sister tilted her head. "Hmm, guess so. It's an old building. I'll get Buck to look at it later. He's a bit preoccupied at the moment. Mr Moorfield's death has really hit him sideways."

I could swear I noticed a knowing glance pass between the sisters. What was obvious was the awkward silence that followed. There's probably been enough talk about Greg Moorfield's death. Time to change the subject.

"So Sis, how's business?"

"The bookshop and cafe are doing well, though it's quieter now, there's still a good demand from the locals. This gaming zone, not so much, but Luke streams games live from here. Sometimes he has several players here competing in worldwide tournaments. They pay him to host events, so whilst the numbers are small, they are loyal and valued customers."

An apologetic smile twitched at the furthest corners of Aunt Pamela's lips. "Sorry, about before. I don't know what came over me." She straightened her torso and shifted herself forward on the settee. "I'm forgetting my manners. Come on, Jess, tell us about Paris."

Finally!

***

The storm had turned the island topsy-turvy whilst I'd been away. Tom and Ernest were acting weird and Pamela was not her usual measured self. Given the worry and strain all three of them were under, that was unsurprising. However, when your anchors are unsteady, it sends ripples throughout the entire sea. I had learnt to see these people as my rocks. Always there, strong and dependable. Now they felt cast adrift. I had fewer points of navigation. The world seemed a scarier place.

This sentiment echoed in the dying remains of Halloween all around me. With the scratchy fingertips of naked tree branches and the biting icy wind, Wesberrey had become a Tim Burton movie set. I half expected Helena Bonham-Carter to jump out and scare me from behind the red post-box on the corner of Market Square as I passed.

But there was nothing and no one to be afraid of. In fact, there was no one about at all. Something was missing. The approaching winter had frightened everyone away. Wesberrey was a lonely, grey place today.

I missed not having Inspector Lovington to bounce ideas around with. His willingness to bend the rules every once in a while made his absence even more keenly felt – just when the family needed him most. DS Stewart would be a much harder nut to crack. Talk of ghostly charades would have little sway with her.

Dave was, on reflection, more open-minded than I had previously given him credit for. If his relationship with my sister was to have any future, he would have to be. Zuzu is my sister, and I adore her, but she is an acquired taste.

How is everything going on at his family estate?

My older sister puts on a convincing show of confidence but that bravado hides a frightened child who wants to please and, above all, be loved. If Dave's mother disapproved of the match, or his children didn't warm to her, she would return heartbroken.

At some point this evening, I need to call her.

I turned right out of Market Square and walked up the hill, as directed by Ernest, to the Victorian villa sporting the ten-foot pole and a forlorn flag. Yesterday's storm had not been kind to Roger Cummings's front garden. As well as the bedraggled Union Jack, the wind had played musical chairs with several plastic tubs and flowerpots. A couple of gnomes were face down in their pond, and the cement windmill ornament behind them had lost a sail.

Despite the carnage, it was easy to see that this was not the normal state of the otherwise immaculate front lawn. The owner of this garden worked hard to maintain its seasonal beauty.

I walked up a red and black diamond tiled path, as original as the villa itself. There were four stone steps up to the front door, with a simple steel railing on the left side. The ceramic tiles under the welcome mat mirrored the black and red diamond theme of the path. The door itself featured ornate glass panels. A white-painted balustrade provided the finishing details to the tall windows on the first floor. It was a beautiful home.

A circular brass plate with a central knob invited me to 'Ring bell - Pull', so I did.

I could hear nothing, so pulled again.

I pressed my ear to the door to listen for any activity inside. Stepping back down a couple of the stone stairs, I looked up at the windows for any signs of life.

I tried again.

"Hold your horses!"

The gravelly voice inside the building came closer and louder.

"Keep your hair on! Everyone is in such a rush these days. No patience. How did they stay in their mother's womb for nine months? I don't know. Maybe they didn't. No discipline from the start."

At the end of this tirade, the door opened a crack, bound in place by a gold-metal chain.

"Oh, a vicar. A lady vicar. Heavens preserve us. What can I do for you? Erm, do I still call you reverend?"

"Absolutely, I'm Reverend Jess Ward. Am I addressing Mr Roger Cummings?"

"Captain Cummings. Yes, you are. How may I help?"

"I wanted to talk to you about Greg Moorfield. I understand you knew him."

"Right. Well, then you had better come in."

Captain Cummings released the chain, and the door opened into a stunning black and white mosaic hallway floor leading to a winding wooden staircase. To the right side stood a wooden sideboard, above which an elaborate gilded mirror proudly hung.

"You have a beautiful home, Captain Cummings. So sorry to see what the storm did to your fabulous garden."

"Hmm, Mother Nature, the biggest litterer of all. At least her detritus is biodegradable," he muttered as we headed towards the kitchen at the back.

He pointed up the stairs as we passed. "The powder room is the first on the left if you need it. No need to ask permission."

He pulled out a red Formica chair with steel legs and gestured for me to take a seat.

"Thank you. I won't take up too much of your time. I don't think I have ever seen you at St Bridget's."

"No," Roger settled himself in another chair at the end of the matching table. The mid-century kitchen set felt strangely at home amidst the late nineteenth-century coving and finials. "And you're not likely to either, Madam Vicar. I don't hold with religion."

There was a portrait of a young Queen Elizabeth II over the fireplace.

"But you are a fan of Her Majesty, I see. How many years did you serve?"

"Twenty years for Queen and country, and proud of it."

"As you should be. Public service is very important. It's good to have pride in where you live. I hear I have you to thank for the litter-free roadsides."

"I'm not in it for the glory. Have enough medals. Don't need any more."

I liked his candour and down-to-earth attitude. Here was a man who believed in getting things done. I doubt he ever took a day off sick or allowed himself to waste a minute of his life in melancholy.

"Well, I appreciate all your hard work, anyway. Now, what can you tell me about Greg Moorfield?"

Porcelain Memories

"To be honest with you, Madam Vicar, I hardly knew the fella. He hung around the squad like a lost puppy. Him and that soppy hound of his. Both as wet as each other. He wanted to gather seaweed to fertilise his garden. Those new plots have negligible nutrients in their soil. Mainly building rubble and sand."

Captain Cummings checked his watch, scratched his nose, and carried on. "Byron took pity on him. You know, he's a big softy, old Byron."

Throughout, Roger sat bolt upright in his chair. No need for slovenliness, even in your own home. Though he wore khaki shorts and a tee-shirt, he'd starched them into crisp lines. I felt like a slob in my drip-dry black trouser and blouse ensemble.

"Yes, Byron is my uncle. He told me a little about the squad. So, from what I remember, there are four of you?"

"You're the twitcher's niece, well I'll be a monkey's uncle. Hey, that's funny." Roger clicked his tongue off the roof of his mouth and looked to the ceiling, "So you're part of that coven, then. Byron was always trying to escape her indoors when the sisters came around. My, my. And you, a lady vicar and all. I don't know what this world is coming to."

"Have you heard my uncle's been arrested?"

Roger screwed up his eyes and forehead. He looked almost neanderthal. "For what?"

I surveyed Roger's features. His confusion appeared genuine. "For the murder of Greg Moorfield."

Roger's raucous laughter filled his pantry kitchen, ricocheting off the hanging copper pans and white ceramic surfaces. "See!" He howled. "The world has gone insane. Completely barking mad!"

"So, you don't think Byron would do this?"

"Tell me Madam Vicar, have you ever killed a man?"

I was confident to offer a hard no to that question.

"Well, I have. It's what they trained me for and still when the time came... When my very life depended on it, I hesitated. One needs more than a stiff upper lip to pull the trigger on someone, even if they are running at you with a machete!"

"I imagine the sawdust dummies in basic training are no match for the real thing."

"Indeed, they are not. They don't have panic in their eyes. Well, they don't have eyes." He used his little joke to ease the tension, for which I was grateful. "Byron may have been in National Service. He's the right age for it. But that's different from active combat. And I hear they shot Moorfield up close between the eyes. That takes a steel stomach and no mistake."

"Or someone with the ability to block out their emotions?" I suggested.

"Or, I would argue, Madam Vicar, someone controlled by them."

I attempted to gain empathy by mirroring Roger's body language, but sitting still wasn't working. The cushion on the vintage chair was more uncomfortable than it looked. My bottom bones found little support, despite my ample personal upholstery, and my cheeks went numb. It's hard to shift your seat without looking awkward or bored, but I had to move.

"Do you mind if I take a closer look at that beautiful portrait of the Queen? Is it from her coronation?"

"Be my guest."

I stretched out my lower limbs with relief and moved over to the mantle. "I was here when her majesty visited for the Silver Jubilee. Were you on the island then?"

"No, I was serving abroad. My aunt presented the bouquet. Dad was so proud of his sister-in-law. He was very patriotic. I suppose he's why I joined the army. There's a picture of her with the Queen from the Stourchestershire Times in the lounge, if you are interested."

"Yes, I am." My brain started joining the memory dots. "Your aunt was the school secretary? Mrs Cummings, right? So, do you have any other relatives on the island?"

The conversation had gone slightly off-topic, but building rapport is a key communication technique. I had to deploy all possible tools if I hoped to save my uncle. Any clue, no matter how small or unwittingly uttered, could be vital to proving his innocence.

"Tons of them. The Cummings have been sowing their seeds on Wesberrey for hundreds of years. We are probably related somewhere along the line."

Roger showed me into a room at the front of the house. I thought I had stepped into a royal palace's gift shop. The Cummings clan had been collecting memorabilia for decades. Glass cabinets lined the walls, shelves full of commemorative plates and mugs celebrating every major royal event for the past hundred years.

I walked around, open-mouthed. "This is quite the collection." My eyes fell on an Edward VIII coronation mug. "This must be rare."

Roger looked over my shoulder. "Oh, everyone thinks that because he abdicated. But in reality, they were planning his coronation and selling merchandise for a long time before he made that decision. They hastily made the plate beside it for the coronation of his brother, George VI. That is worth a fortune."

"So who was the collector?"

"It was just something we did. My grandparents probably started it. I have thought about selling them. They're a bugger to dust. eBay, maybe. Meacham has a store online."

"That would be Paul Meacham. He's one of your squad, right?"

"Yeah, he's not bad for a peace-loving hippie. He has a good eye for beach treasure. Makes a pretty good living from his finds. Driftwood and sea glass are big earners right now."

"So Paul doesn't need the money then, from a bigger find, such as a lump of ambergris?"

I noticed Roger's facial expression shift in the cabinet door's reflection. The mention of the whale vomit had hit a nerve.

"Oh, so you heard about that." He backed away. I turned to follow him to the sofa.

"Yes, Byron told me. But DS Stewart appears to be unaware of it. Which is interesting, isn't it? I assume the police have interviewed you all."

"We all swore not to tell anyone until we had it valued." Roger hung his head in his hands.

"Even after one of you was killed?"

"Moorfield wasn't really one of us. Anyway, the two things aren't connected. My theory is that it was a terrible accident."

"They shot him between the eyes. How is that an accident?"

"Or friendly fire."

Is this guy for real?

"Surely, Captain Cummings, you must think it's suspicious that your squad found a valuable piece of ambergris, and that night the man who discovered it had an accident with a nail gun in your shared beach hut."

"Wait, you surely don't think I am a suspect?" Roger stood up and marched towards the lounge door. "I think it's time for you to leave, Madame Vicar."

I walked over to the framed press cutting on the fire's mantelpiece. "May I?"

He nodded.

"I remember your aunt. Family is important. I believe my uncle is innocent and the police have stopped looking for any other suspects. The ambergris has to be a potential motive. Where is it now?"

"In Moorfield's house, I would imagine. He took it home with him. After all, he found it."

"Finders keepers. I guess that's a rule of beachcombing."

"Well, I can't speak for other combers, but it was a rule for the squad. We are all honourable men, even Meacham. He's a pacifist, but at least he has a moral code."

"I need to meet him. And Kenneth Wilson? He's the other member of your group. What's he like?"

"I think you should find out for yourself. Madam Vicar, if you need someone to vouch for my moral character..." He pointed at an open box next to the framed press cutting. "And the medals in that case there stand for nothing. Talk to my cousin Rosemary. She's one of your flock."

"Rosemary Reynolds?"

"Nee Cummings, yes. The school secretary you remember so fondly is her mother."

He Sells Seashells

Next on the agenda was this evening's dinner party. I called Luke on his mobile to find out what people might want to eat, only to be told not to worry. He and Tilly had it covered. I did not know what that meant, but sometimes one has to trust that others can sort things out on their own.

Roger had given me addresses for the other members of the beach squad and with my uncle languishing in a cement cell at Her Majesty's pleasure and my aunt crumbling into a deconstructed Eton Mess, I set off to visit the first name on the list - Paul Meacham.

Kenneth Wilson's house was on the far side of the island and without Cilla, he would have to wait until tomorrow. My image of Mr Wilson was confusing. Byron called him a spiv and yet Roger Cummings said they were all honourable men.

Perhaps Mr Meacham, who lived on Back Lane, a couple of hundred yards away from the vicarage, could shed more light on Mr Wilson's character.

The houses on Back Lane were humble nineteenth-century two-up, two-down workers' homes. When Wesberrey had a thriving port, these simple terraced buildings provided lodging to the dockhands working in Harbour Parade and Stone Quay.

The island's position off the coast had awarded it a steady trade as a gateway to the southeast of England for centuries. Later train travel, road haulage and air cargo alternatives provided direct routes to the capital and home counties, leading to the harbour's slow demise after the first world war.

When the navy finally left in the sixties, most of the islanders had to find work on the mainland and gradually the population changed. Old families left, to be replaced in more recent years by people coming to Wesberrey seeking a slice of the old ways. The once deprived areas with idling houses saw a building frenzy. Some newcomers commute, but most work remotely or from home. Young families with professional, artistic or techy bent seeking a slower and safer way of life.

Sadly, this increase in population did not correlate with an increase in church attendance.

I had heard Paul Meacham was an artist, and the front of his abode did not disappoint. He filled his small front yard with colourful painted terracotta pots oozing with ivy trails and winter pansies. A cement figurine of the Venus de Milo covered in a mosaic of blue and green sea glass pebbles held on her head a matching bird table. She offered fresh water for her feathered friends, whilst a statue of Michelangelo's David, clothed in seashells, provided seeds.

Under the bay window, on a rusty yellow-painted wooden garden seat, sat a bearded man I took to be the owner.

"I'm looking for Paul Meacham?"

"Well, looks like you found him. And you are?"

"Reverend Jessamy Ward. I'm the parish priest of St Bridget's"

"Ah, so are you on the hunt for new recruits? Well, don't waste your time here, Vicar. Confirmed agnostic, if there is such a thing. Leaning more towards atheism than monotheism. Dabbled in Buddhism, but then, haven't we all?"

He raised a rolled cigarette to his lips and inhaled, puffing out a ring of smoke with a distinctly unpleasant woody odour.

He saw my nose twitch.

"Do you want some?" he asked.

"Er, no thank you. I'm on duty."

Paul snorted. "What can I do for you?"

"I was talking to your friend, Roger Cummings, earlier about the Beach Squad. Byron is my uncle."

"Ah, yes. I think he mentioned that once." Paul took another drag.

"Well, the police have him in custody for the murder of Greg Moorfield, and —"

Paul choked and beat his chest as if to dislodge the shock. "Byron? Sorry, Vicar, but that is the funniest thing I have heard in forever."

"Glad you find it amusing. Do you mind if I ask you a few questions?"

Mr Meacham sucked the end of his roll-up and then flicked it into a nearby pot. "Don't worry, it's completely organic. Come inside. Looks like it's going to rain."

Paul's home on the inside echoed the colourful chaos of its exterior. He packed every conceivable surface with books or artist tools. Canvases in gangs of three or more rested against cupboard doors, walls or even further piles of books. By the fireplace stood a pile of driftwood finds and on the far table beneath a window, through which I could make out a narrow passage to a small paved backyard, sat glass bowls with different coloured glass pebbles.

"My uncle told me you have an eBay store. That you sell your beach finds online."

"Etsy. I have an Etsy store," he huffed. "I create art from the offerings of the sea gods."

He handed me a business card.

"Ah, I see 'Triton's Trash'. Great alliteration. So. Greek gods are fine. It's just mine you have an issue with."

"You know your mythology. I am impressed. I studied Greek literature as part of my degree. Mainly the plays. Aeschylus, Sophocles, and Euripides."

A few familiar titles popped from the books on the shelf closest to me. "We studied Medea and Electra at drama school."

"Ah, you were a thespian. Interesting career change."

Paul moved a pile of dusty books from a plain wooden chair and invited me to sit. He rested his rear on the arm of a nearby sofa. It was the only part of the couch not overflowing with newspaper and bubble wrap.

"Yes, years ago. I saw Diana Rigg at the Almeida. The early nineties, I think."

"Oh, so did I. She was magnificent. Now you had questions about Byron. Not sure what I can tell you about your uncle that you don't already know."

You'd be surprised.

"I understand you are both members of the Beach Squad alongside Captain Cummings and Kenneth Wilson. Greg Moorfield was a new member and had only been beach-combing with you a couple of times."

"That is correct. Though I think you'll find that Captain Cummings is getting ideas above his rank. Word is the highest he got to was sergeant. I'm sure that is something that anyone with a bit of internet savvy could verify."

A rustling sound came from under the table by the window, and then a small pile of papers toppled over.

Is it a rat?

I gripped the edge of my chair as if that somehow would save me from a pack of vicious rodents hungry for blood. My blood.

Paul Meacham was unperturbed.

Do rats seek blood or am I thinking of bats?

Biting down on my desire to scream and run, I pursued the next obvious question.

"What makes you think Roger Cummings is lying?"

"Oh, something Wilson once said. They were arguing over a game of dominoes in the hut, and Cummings ripped into Wilson about having only done National Service and then being nothing more interesting than an accountant after demob. And Wilson threw back that at least he wasn't delusional and making out to everyone else that he was an officer."

"And you and my uncle weren't part of that conversation?"

"Nah, Byron and I knew better than to get between them when they started old army tales. Your uncle did his National Service in the navy. Ex-army don't have any issue with them, and National Service was all over by the time I turned eighteen. I'm the baby of the bunch. What a difference a few years make. I grew up with the full benefits of a grammar school education and a free ticket to university."

"And what did you do after you graduated?"

"What do most English Lit graduates do? I went into teaching. I travelled the world. Spent some time in India, Thailand, and Singapore. Taught Shakespeare to the ex-pat community. Retired here to write my novel and discovered a love for art instead."

"Why Wesberrey? I detect a London accent."

"Cheap housing and remoteness. I toyed with the idea of buying a croft in the Scottish Highlands, but you have to tend the land, and I don't really do manual labour."

"So, you have made a successful business from the beach. Must have galled a bit when Greg Moorfield found the biggest sea prize of all?"

"You mean the ambergris?" Paul's forehead contorted into a pretzel. "He didn't find it. His dog did. Why would that be an issue? Moorfield had agreed to share the profits with his new best friends."

Dinner At The Vicarage

I stopped at the cemetery on the way back. The lilac-or-ange of twilight provided enough light to guide my way. Thinking I had brought up their evening meal, the Wesberrey clowder gathered around me as I walked. They emerged from root mounds and piles of fallen leaves like camouflaged special operatives. Slinking behind and between headstones as they weaved their way to the gathering place under the old oak.

I left them there whilst I continued to the vicarage to fetch their supper.

Chicken in gravy with carrots tonight, I think.

The kitchen light illuminated my last few steps across the back garden. Through the window, I could see Luke and Tilly dancing around the table, laying out cutlery for our meal. How Tilly had transformed my nephew from a miserable, apathetic teen into a playful young man was testimony to the power of love. Young love is most intoxicating.

Behind them by the cupboards, Rosie and Buck were nuzzling up together as they prepared the plates. Discovering love in later life is equally fulfilling.

Love, in all its disguises, is an unstoppable force.

I should have invited Lawrence. I'm going to be the spare wheel times two.

I grabbed the cat food and trays from the wood store at the back of the vicarage and carefully walked back to my feline friends. They circled around me as I served their dinner. Some new kittens, their eyes barely open, slunk in under their mothers' bellies, curious what all the fuss was about. The approaching winter would not treat these babies kindly.

Note to self: parish notice for spare crates and blankets.

I turned on the torch on my phone to navigate my way back through fallen branches and grave markers. The sodden ground dragged at my shoes. My feet lifted heavier with every step. A home-cooked meal would help restore my energy, but I wasn't looking forward to a night of quizzing and theorising, no matter how entertaining the company.

Every bone ached with exhaustion, though my mind was buzzing.

So many questions, and zero answers.

I steeled myself and opened the back door.

There was another familiar face in the kitchen I had missed through the window earlier. Lawrence was kneeling on the floor, engaged in a futile conversation with the lofty Hugo. My earnest fiancé was encouraging the furry fusspot to try his bowl of kibble bites.

"He won't touch those whilst there are potential scraps from the table. Let him be. He'll go back afterwards."

Lawrence abandoned his position at the food station and stood up for a welcome home kiss.

Through force of habit, I hesitated for a moment. Public displays of our emotions had not been our thing. The momentary rejection in his blue eyes stabbed deep. My penitent left thumb wiggled the band of the beautiful ring Lawrence had placed on my wedding finger less than forty-eight hours before.

No need for caution anymore.

I pulled his face back towards mine and planted a firm confirmation of my love on his lips.

"It's so good to see you here," I whispered.

His lips brushed mine a second time. Then he pivoted me around to face our guests.

"We've set a date," he announced. "December twenty-sixth."

"Boxing Day?" Rosie gasped.

Everyone offered their congratulations.

Even Alfie rose from his slumber in front of the aga cooker and weaved his way into the celebrations. His toasty cream body wrapped itself around my freezing legs.

Hugo remained unimpressed, but I knew he would warm to the idea later.

I am the one who feeds him, after all.

***

"That was delicious." I patted my full stomach in appreciation. "Lentil casserole proved to be much nicer than it sounds. And this bread is gorgeous."

Rosie beamed, "Yes, I picked it up from the Needhams on the way up. Along with their good wishes for Aunt Pamela. Seems Uncle Byron used to pop in every morning for a fresh bloomer."

"Did he? But, he never visited your shop?"

"Not since the opening." She sighed.

Buck offered an explanation. "Maybe he thought it off-limits. We men are primitive creatures, you know. We like our caves and sacred places to retreat to. Like his beach hut or the shed. If Byron saw your cafe as somewhere where the womenfolk meet, man, he would avoid it like the plague."

Buck's Texan drawl always made everything sound so authoritative. Like he pulled his knowledge from the bygone wisdom of his cowboy ancestors.

I looked to Lawrence to confirm or deny.

"Hmm, I think we all need our own space from time to time."

Luke was eager to join in. "It's like my gaming den in the shop. Yeah, we have girl gamers, but it's the guys who hire out our space. That need to close out the world and re-energise is strong."

Buck snapped his fingers over the breadbasket. "Yes, that's it right there. Men seek out dens to regroup or lick their wounds. Women find energy in sharing. Coming together. Supporting each other. Men need a time-out."

"But women want that too." Rosie refilled her glass of water. "A soak in the bath, alone, at the end of a hard day is bliss."

I raised my glass. "Amen to that."

Tilly tore a piece of bread off and used it to mop up the sauce in her bowl. "Men just need to get away from their wives and their mundane lives. Hobbies, sports, clubs. They can't just gather for a chat. They have to have a purpose, an excuse. The more desperate they are, the more extreme the outlet."

I reflected on Tilly's insight. She had already lived so much life. "Okay, the Beach Squad was an excuse to escape from the monotony of their lives once or twice a week."

Buck nodded. "Yes, ma'am, like a book club with practical applications."

"Oh, that reminds me." Rosie swallowed before her announcement. "We're starting a book club at D and V in the new year. I can get the books in at cost, sell at a discount to the members and make my money on the food and beverages. Hopefully, once through the door, they will buy other books too."

"Sis, that sounds like a great idea. You might need to get that leak checked out first." I squeezed her hand and nodded in the general direction of her beau. "So, much like a book club, the Beach Squad's weekly meetings united these men in their desire to escape, rather than a desire for friendship?"

Buck looked at the other men around the table. "Yup. From what we know about them so far, they don't sound like sworn comrades in arms. I'd say they'd turn on each other faster than a prairie fire with a tailwind. I'll be curious to know what you find out about what's his name? Kenneth Wilson? Is he a low-level hustler or lonely hobbyist?"

"After dinner, I think we should put everything we know on the board." Tilly jumped in her chair. "I'll scribe. I can file summaries of your conversations in the folders, whilst Luke joins up the dots with the woollen thread."

Rosie pushed herself away from the table and lifted the kettle off its stand. "I'll make the coffee. Buck, why don't you tell Jess what you found out on your walk earlier?"

"Yes, ma'am. I know poor old Greg used to take Alfie here for a walk along the shoreline same time every morning. He was a creature of habit. Friday was always wash day. He was the only neighbour to put his underwear on a line in his backyard."

Buck sat back in his chair and folded his arms across his chest, and smiled. "Now that's a strange little British custom I still find perplexing. No one would do that back home for fear of being strung up themselves by the residents' housing association."

"But, Dad, we don't have a residents' association."

"And that, my beautiful gal, is also strange. People can put whatever they want on their front lawns and no one pays any mind."

I tried to rein in the conversation. I had a warm bed calling my name, and it was getting late.

"So, let's go back. You took Alfie for a walk at what time?"

"That would have been around eight."

"And Mr Moorfield walked Alfie at the same time every day?"

"Yes, ma'am. He did the same the day he died. Walked Alfie at eight. I saw him from the bedroom window. Greg took him down the limestone path that runs to the beach. Then usually, he takes him across to the park around six-thirty in the evening for a quick run. Lots of dog walkers gather there after work to allow their pups to let off a little steam before settling in for the night."

"Right. So he only walks Alfie on the beach in the morning. Do we know if he walked him again that evening? Any witnesses?" I asked.

"Funny you should say that." Buck sat forward, his brow furrowed. "There was this one woman, ponytail, horsey type. She thanked me for taking Alfie on. She was worried after she didn't see him at the park with Greg the night before and then she heard the news."

Luke reverted into full schoolboy mode, sticking his hand excitedly in the air, looking fit to burst.

"I think my nephew has an idea. Share away". I waved his entry into the conversation.

"Right. Yes. Well. That means that Mr Moorfield was already dead by six o'clock, six thirty at the latest."

Buck patted my nephew on the back. "I think you've got something there, son."

Tilly smoothed down the paper she was writing on and drew a line across the page. "We need a timeline. Okay..." She drew a short vertical line intersecting the first line on the left-hand side.

"We know Mr Moorfield walked Alfie around eight a.m. on the beach, but he didn't walk him later at six-thirty." She drew another short line at the end on the right. "We need to track his movements in between. We know who the suspects are. Now we have to establish who had the motive and opportunity."

"This is really useful. Okay, gang, I need to speak to Kenneth Wilson. Buck, can you let me into Greg's house to snoop around? And we've got to gain access to the beach hut. Should I join you on Alfie's walk in the morning?"

"Sounds fine by me, Reverend."

A silence fell over the group. Everyone wanted to be a part of this, and only Buck and I were free to investigate during the day. The troops needed some motivation.

"We'll meet here again tomorrow night and share what we've learnt, okay?" I assured them.

Rosie ended the conversation with a firm deployment of steaming coffee. "Perfect timing. Let's take these upstairs quickly and fill in that board you were talking about. We all have an early start in the morning."

Man's Best Friend

The late evening injection of caffeine had failed to register. Sensing that I was bone-tired, Lawrence went home when the others left. I love them all deeply, and we were working on something extremely important, but my mind and body were grateful for an hour's peace before heading up to bed.

Drained of all thought and feeling, I should have gone straight to bed, but I needed to retreat to my cave. Listen to some music, read something. Unwind. Zone-out.

I also needed to check in with the Big Guy Upstairs.

Despite the gloom hanging over the family, I offered a prayer of gratitude. I thanked my heavenly Boss for the gifts I had received, whatever their provenance. All things in the universe stem from Him. It is for us to decide whether to use them for good or ill.

I asked Him to send me the wisdom to utilise my abilities to the fullest as I endeavoured to find out who killed Greg Moorfield. For the truth to be unveiled, and justice to be done.

In the kitchen, I could hear Hugo finishing his kibble.

Time to climb the wooden hill to sleepy town.

***

Morning broke through my curtains. The trees outside teemed with flocks of migrating birds on their way to sunnier climates. Their busy chatter drowned out the soft coos of the resident collared doves. When the breeze picked up and shook the bird-filled branches, their conversation subsided, only to return to full volume when the trees calmed down.

It was a glorious day for my morning stroll with Alfie. And Buck, obviously.

I am a dog person at heart. *Don't tell Hugo*. Perhaps I should think about getting a canine companion. Maybe not a golden retriever, something small and feisty to counter Hugo's aloofness. A terrier, perhaps. *Jack Russells are cute, or a Chihuahua?*

Alfie was a walking mustard-coloured shag pile rug. Considering he had just lost his master, Alfie was easy-going and loving with everyone, even Hugo. The night before he had blended into the furniture so well, we only remembered he was there when his tail drummed the floor or our legs in excitement, or his rear produced some noxious fumes. Which it did several times.

Dogs are more smelly and muddy. They need walks and...

Buck was waiting for me on the pavement outside his house. Alfie, a good boy by his side. "Okay, ma'am. I say we take the exact route poor old Greg took that day and start from his backyard. I've brought the keys. We go in through the house and return there for a snoop around later."

"There's no police cordon or blue and white tape?" I couldn't contain my shock. Dave would never allow such sloppy police work. Though a tape wouldn't stop anyone, it's true. Like a birthday message on Facebook, it's the thought that counts. I suspected very little thought was going into this investigation.

"I don't think they have been near the place." Buck unlocked Greg's front door. "Well, that's to say, I haven't seen anyone. Strange, eh, Jess? I guess they figured they have their man. Byron's prints are on the murder weapon. They have the body and where he died. No need to check out anywhere else."

"But they don't have a mo-." My words were whisked away as Alfie led the charge through his former home, sniffing for fresh scents as he went. His tail bashed back and forth like a loose gate in a hurricane.

"Hey, boy! Have you found something?" Buck released Alfie's lead, and the retriever shot into the lounge. "I think we should follow."

I agreed.

Buck bounded down the hallway, following Alfie as he ricocheted from room to room. I took a more sedate pace, running my fingers over surfaces, hoping for helpful paranormal insights.

Alfie's frantic energy soon descended into a mournful whimper.

"Ah, perhaps he's looking for his master." I sighed.

Greg Moorfield's sparsely decorated bungalow was much as I expected. The walls remained the generic magnolia and white colour new builds always have. Beige medium pile carpets ran throughout, even in the bathroom. *A very British quirk.* Only the kitchen had a hard floor, a simple tile effect vinyl covering in blue and white squares.

His furniture was mid to late twentieth-century scandic oak. Two faded orange and chocolate brown winged-back chairs with matching footstools provided the only hint of colour. A tattered sofa ran along the back wall doing its best to hold court to three antique gold and scarlet embroidered cushions. A few eclectic pieces of objet d'art sat on the window ledge. I was drawn to the ceramic head with line-drawn areas on the scalp. I saw one once in a parish jumble and thought it the strangest thing. A series of Constable reproductions hung too high in their oak frames, and on the mantle above the real-flame gas fire rested a pair of Royal Doulton porcelain posies of roses in white three-legged bowls.

In the centre, under a plain wooden mirror, stood two framed photographs. A black-and-white photograph of his wedding day in one and a picture of the loving couple with their son in the other. The fashion and colouration suggested they took the picture in the early to mid-seventies.

In fact, it was hard to believe this was a twenty-first-century new-build home, I felt I had stepped back in time to the early Seventies.

Must be treasured possessions from when Mr and Mrs Moorfield first set up home. Not much to show for seventy-odd years on this planet.

Alfie howled at the back door. Even he knew that the best cure for depression is fresh air. It was time for his walk. Further investigation would have to wait until we returned.

Buck fastened Alfie's lead to his collar, and I locked up.

"Do we know if the police have notified his son yet?" I asked.

"They must've, surely? I mean, just because I haven't seen them in the house doesn't mean they haven't been there. Though, you have to agree PC Taylor is a bit slow-witted. Keen as a week-old piglet, but lacking any horse sense."

"I couldn't possibly comment, but the house looked immaculate. The police aren't known for their careful searches. Would they take photos? If they don't think it's a crime scene, I mean."

Buck's feet skidded down the chalk path. He slipped and tripped behind the excited retriever. "I guess you'll just have to ask a policeman. Shame we don't know any, eh?"

"I doubt I will be popular if I call Dave about police procedure whilst he's on holiday."

I trotted down the path, which was much steeper than it looked. Catch a toe on a raised rock or tuft of grass and I would end up rolling down the hill.

Alfie stopped to smell a present left by one of his canine friends.

Dogs have disgusting habits.

I pulled up alongside Buck, who had taken advantage of Alfie's break to admire the coastline before us.

"It's a mighty fine vista we have here, isn't it?"

This side of the island looked out over the North Sea. The sunsets from the beach below are legendary.

"Greg Moorfield walked Alfie down here every day? And back up again?" I turned to face the steep descent we had just travelled down. "He must've been very fit for his age."

"He looked after himself, that's for sure. Plenty of years left in him, if he hadn't... Well, you know what I mean."

Buck stroked his new best friend's golden coat. "Hey, boy. If I let you off the lead, will you run away?"

Alfie's slobbery mouth panted into a smile.

"I think that's a no." I laughed.

Dogs are full of drool, but also full of character. Maybe I will get one?

Free from his ties, Alfie bounced ahead down to the beach, pausing every few seconds to check we were following behind.

A few minutes later, we were strolling along the concrete curved wall that protected the crumbling coastline from further sea erosion. This side of the island had flooded during a severe storm in the fifties, and they erected this ugly wall to protect nearby properties. Every so often there are reports of houses collapsing off the cliff's edge nearby. When the council granted planning permission for the new estate, many locals protested. Structural engineers confirmed there was no risk, and the building went ahead.

Quick prayer to the Big Guy that everyone who lives there would remain safe in their homes.

The wall led to a row of brightly painted beach huts. Each had stairs and a small veranda to the front. Some featured nautical or sea-related decorations on their exteriors, whilst others were plain and unadorned. One stood out from the pack, clearly distinguished by the trailing 'Police - Do Not Cross' tapes fluttering in the breeze.

Ah, well at least the police have been here!

"I guess that's Byron's," I pointed up ahead. "Looks like Alfie recognises it too."

The faithful pup had curled himself into a breakfast croissant on the porch in front of the door. He jumped up as soon as we approached and began scratching at the bottom panel.

I looked around, and the beach was empty. "Shame we don't have a key."

Buck produced Greg's front door keys from his pocket. "There's a bunch of them here, worth a try."

Eliminating the keys to the front and back doors of Greg's house, left two other options. The first looked like it belonged to a filing cabinet or small box, but the second...

"Vicar, throw your hat over the windmill. We're in!"

The Scent of a Clue

The beach hut was a cosy seven-by-seven-foot square, just big enough to house a table and chairs and store the group's beachcombing equipment. They hung some of their finds from pegs on the wooden slats. Other treasures were on a small plank shelf that doubled as a worktop or in boxes stacked to the side. The space was efficient and practical. There were no soft furnishings or nods to home comforts.

A paraffin cooking stove and a lamp provided heating and light. The aesthetic was rudimentary, militaristic, and functional. Buck appeared impressed.

"Now this is a club I might wanna be part of."

"Really? Isn't it a bit... sparse?" I picked up a mini hacksaw from the worktop.

Buck examined the paraffin lamp. "What else do ya need? I guess they come with provisions. There's a pan down there, they can cook up some beans."

I opened the lid of a corner box, "Or make some porridge, there's a box of oatmeal in here."

"Mmm-huh, a pretty nice little setup, if you ask me."

"Buck, there are lots of dangerous tools here. Any of them could have been used to kill Moorfield and thrown into the sea afterwards. Why choose the nail gun?"

"I see what you are saying. Why leave it behind for the cops to find?"

"Exactly, unless you wanted to cast suspicion elsewhere? That suggests to me this was premeditated. The killer planned everything in advance."

I caught Buck's face in a small mirror hung by a twill thread from a nail on the wall. There was a definite curl to the corners of his lips. He was enjoying this.

"And where's the blood? Or any signs of a struggle?" I continued.

"They discovered his body outside, so that must have been where he died. It clearly wasn't inside the hut." Buck left the hut in search of further clues. "Do we know who found him?"

I followed to look for traces of blood. *Maybe a nail gun to the forehead doesn't leave much of a trail?*

Nothing. The storm and subsequent showers must have washed them away.

Maybe if I quieten my mind...

Alfie's snout nudged my right hand.

"Shush, boy. I am trying to focus."

He licked my fingers, then turned and ran about in small circles, on each return spin, coming back briefly to bop my hand with the top of his head.

Buck's voice boomed over my shoulder. "Have you never watched Lassie? He wants you to follow him."

I shrugged. "Where? There's nothing here, only pebbles and sand."

Alfie revved up his rear end, using his tail to lead the way as he reversed towards the incoming tide. Then he stopped. As we drew closer, he pawed at the ground beneath him, speaking to us in repeated bursts of three barks to one growl.

Buck pulled Alfie back by his collar and lavished the fluffy detective with praise. "Something's buried here? Who's a clever boy."

Alfie lapped up the opportunity for a belly rub and rolled over on his back. It delighted Buck to oblige. Greg's dog had found a wonderful new home.

"Right, well, let's see what's hiding here." I nipped back to the beach hut to pick up a miniature spade.

I dug where Alfie suggested. The rains had compacted the wet sand beneath into soft, grainy clay, making it hard to remove.

I went down about six inches and didn't find anything. *This could be a lot of effort for a large amount of nothing.*

I carried on. Buck amused Alfie with a washed-up stick. Several rounds of fetch later, the tip of the spade hit something metal.

"Buck! Come here!"

I dug around the sides. Whatever it was, it measured at least a foot wide. My wrists ached and my fingertips were blue with the cold.

"Hand that tool over, ma'am. You go amuse Alfie. I've got this."

We swapped places. The lolloping golden retriever was just as happy with his new playmate, fortunately. He wiggled around on his back, his pink tongue flopping out the side of his jaw.

Where does he get his energy from?

"It's a box!" Buck yelled from over the trench.

He lifted out a locked grey metal chest with two side handles.

"I bet that contains the infamous ambergris." I knelt beside our find and brushed off the residual sand.

"And what are the odds on this key fitting that lock?"

Alfie dropped his stick toy at my feet and collapsed beside us, panting hard.

I cast a nervous eye to either side. "He needs a drink. Perhaps we should take this back to Greg's house to open it. Who knows who's watching us?" In the distance, a couple of dog walkers, maybe wary of trampling over a crime scene, had stayed away from this end of the beach. Which was fortunate for us, but made me feel a tad guilty.

We should tell PC Taylor at least.

The simple command 'Home' from Buck had Alfie bounding back towards the pathway. His new master locked up the hut and followed behind us, carrying the box. The precarious walk down was now a tough climb back up. The incline worked my calf muscles to the point of breaking.

I turned to survey my achievement at the summit. "Guess it gets easier if one does it every day." I puffed.

"You should try it with a heavy load sometime." Buck laughed.

"Sorry, let's get into the house."

***

Fed and watered, Alfie wandered into the front room, paced in a circle on the rug in front of the fire, and collapsed – a panting wreck of fur and happiness.

"I guess that's his spot."

"Well, do you want to do the honours?" Buck handed me Greg's keys.

"Perhaps we should have left it there? Reported it to the police?"

"And say what?" Buck broke into a strong Dick Van Dyke cockney accent. "I'm sorry Inspector, but we broke into that there hut to look for clues to exonerate my uncle and then happened upon this here box."

"Something like that, yeah."

"Jess, the police weren't even looking for this. And, if it is the ambergris, that still doesn't prove your uncle didn't do it. He could have put it there to cover his tracks. Or

Greg hid it before he killed him, and Byron just didn't have time to go back to get it before he was arrested. Did they all know it was there? Did the killer? Maybe Greg took that little secret to his grave. It proves nothing and... it might even be empty, though it's darn heavy for an empty box."

I dusted off the lock and fiddled with the keys.

"Erm, Buck. I don't think any of these will work."

He snatched them back. "Are you sure?" Buck tried each one in the lock with no success.

He lifted up a brass Yale key. "Front door."

Next was a long silver Chubb key with an oval at one end and staggered teeth at the bottom. "Back door."

"This opened the shed, so this one has to open ..." Buck tried again. The key was too small.

"You're right, this doesn't prove Byron didn't do it. We can't even prove it belonged to Greg Moorfield." I rubbed my forehead.

Why do humans do that? Rub the front of their brains like that action will activate some secret knowledge held deep within. All it did was smooth out my worry lines, temporarily.

"Buck, you might think this is a little weird, but I'm going to try something."

I pulled the box towards me across Greg's kitchen table and wrapped my hands around it. "Can you record me? Or take down anything I say. In fact, it might help if you ask me questions."

Buck obediently pulled out his phone.

I was becoming too accustomed to stuff like this. Getting into the zone was easier each time. I had asked God to help me use my gifts. I had to trust that he would come through.

"So, what's supposed to happen?" he asked.

"It takes a few seconds." The metal sides of the box felt sharp. Parts of the rusty edges flaked under my fingers. I squeezed my eyes tighter together and concentrated as hard as I could.

"I can see myself burying the box. My hands are crepey, male, I think. Veiny. No nail polish. Smooth, though. The wind is beating the sand into my eyes. There must be a storm brewing. I need to get back."

"Woohoo! Reverend, this voodoo is blowing my mind. Is there anyone else with you?"

"No. I don't think so. It's getting late. I need to be quick. Still so much to do to prepare. I have to get back before they arrive. "

"Who? Before who arrives?"

"The others. It's a game. I like puzzles. It will help to pass the time." I answered.

"That's not at all cryptic."

I tried to block out his cynicism.

My senses were in overdrive. The smells of the coastline fought for my attention. Seaweed, saltwater, diesel. And is that candyfloss? I could hear Buck scratching his head. His scalp dry beneath his fingernails.

"Shush, there's a sound. Someone is here. Walking behind me." I focused on the footsteps, but they stopped.

"I'm covering the box up. Seaweed, bladderwrack I think - the brown one with the bubbles, and a large shell to mark the spot. And a stick. I am inserting a small stick in the sand."

This has to be Greg Moorfield's residual memory. How does it work? I don't know.

"Standing up now. Dusting the sand off my trousers. Can I smell candy floss? Children. Dressed for Halloween, bless them. So sweet at that age... Wait, no, not young children. That's not right?"

High-pitched whimpering noises came from the lounge, breaking my concentration.

"Don't worry, Alfie's having a dream. Sometimes he looks like he's running, it's so cute." Buck assured me. "He was terribly excited about this box, though. It must have belonged to Greg."

"Yes, probably. Did you get all that?"

Buck nodded. "Wasn't the most strenuous task of the morning." He switched off his phone's recorder. "So, no names. No faces? Not sure how this helps us, but..." Buck was taking all this in his stride, like recording the local vicar channelling a dead guy in their kitchen was a normal, everyday occurrence. "One thing, though, what is candy floss?"

"I think you yanks call it cotton candy?"

"Ah, got ya. You mentioned it was a game? Could this be a Halloween prank that went horribly wrong?"

"Who knows?" I pushed the box back into the middle of the table. "What I do know is that I can't do this alone. I need help. We were going to meet again at mine tonight, right? Let's gather at yours instead. We need to search this place from top to bottom."

"That plan works for me. So what are you going to do for the rest of the day?"

"Find Kenneth Wilson."

Byron's Your Uncle

F irst, I had to go back to the vicarage to get Cilla and grab something quick to eat. Psychic channelling was hungry work, and the results so far did not convince me it was worth the extra calories.

Do we know more than I think?

Greg buried the box as part of a game, maybe a treasure hunt, perhaps the killer ran out of clues, or patience. And the stick to mark the spot? I don't recall that being there. Maybe Alfie knocked it over. Or the sea took it away. I suppose it was only meant to be a temporary marker.

The question is, do we try to find the clues and follow the game through to the end or pick the lock and jump to the final square. Does the game matter, or is the prize the key? And has either anything to do with why someone shot Greg Moorfield between the eyes with a nail gun?

So many unanswered questions. Why use the nail gun? To implicate my uncle. Surely, Byron wouldn't use his own tool as a weapon, and certainly not one with his name on it. Why kill Greg Moorfield outside the beach hut and leave him there for any passing dog walker or costumed child to find? Was the killer interrupted? Did they panic, or was it all premeditated?

I should have opened the box. Its contents will tell us more than any stupid psychic hoodoo claptrap.

Barbara was busy updating records in the parish filing cabinet when I arrived.

"Any news on your uncle?" she asked with her head buried in the A-E drawer.

"Not yet. I will pop over to my aunt's this afternoon to check in on her." I flopped into my office chair. "Barbara, what is everyone saying? This must be the talk of the Cat and Fiddle."

"You know me, Reverend. Never one to spread idle gossip."

My exhaustion beat an escape path from my mouth in the heaviest of exhalations. "Does everyone believe he did it?"

My ever-faithful secretary slammed the drawer shut and stood, arms crossed, in silhouette against the light of the noon sun.

"Don't be daft. There is a sweepstake running behind the bar, though. Odds-on favourite at the moment is Ken Wilson."

The revelation that the locals were taking bets on the murderer shocked me bolt upright. "Why do they think it's one of the Beach Squad?"

Barbara bristled. "Well, it happened outside their hut. The police arrested your uncle, so the rest of that motley gang of old men must be suspects. That new DS mentioned the nail gun. I told her over her poached egg and fried mushrooms she needed to cast her net wider. Headstrong woman, that one, Reverend and no mistake."

"So, none of you think Byron did it?"

"Of course not. He's the only one of them anyone likes. Ken Wilson is a total curmudgeon. Paul Meacham and his so-called art, what is that all about, I ask you? There's a man in need of a rub down with a cold loofah. And as for Roger Cummings, with his litter patrols, thinks he's a cut above the rest of us, if you know what I mean?"

"I don't understand why the police aren't looking at them, too? To my knowledge, they haven't even interviewed them."

"She said there was a witness."

The sun moved behind a cloud and for a moment I could see my parish secretary's face. Her expression told me all I needed to know. Someone had seen my uncle kill Greg Moorfield. I believe basketball fans would call that a slam dunk.

"Who?"

"Now that I can't tell you, because I don't know. It's a shame Inspector Lovington is on holiday. No disrespect, Reverend, but your uncle needs some real help if he's going to get out of this."

I agreed.

***

"Zuzu, I'm glad you are having a lovely time, and the jacuzzi in your room sounds delightful, but I really need to speak to Dave."

I had tried to ring the inspector on his mobile phone first, but he didn't answer. Ten minutes into my conversation with my sister I learnt it was because he was out horse riding with his children. Zuzu had decided horses weren't her style and was enjoying a spa moment instead.

"Barbara thinks there's a witness who can place Byron on the scene, nail gun in hand."

"Have you tried your witchy thing with the nail gun? Hold on..." In the background, I could make out muted sounds of bathwater breaching the top of the tub and the padding of wet feet on marble tiles. "That's better, I was starting to wrinkle. Jessie, just talk to PC Taylor. Smile at him pretty, and he will be putty in your hands."

I am not flirting with PC Taylor!

"The nail gun is in the evidence room in Stourchester. Can't you ask Dave to find out who the witness is?"

"Of course I will, but you know he gets all official procedure about these things. It's kinda cute."

My sister can be frustrating, and my impatience showed. "Zuzu, this is our uncle!"

"I know. Don't you think I am worried sick as well? You don't have the monopoly on compassion, you know."

"I'm sorry, but I could really do with your help like before."

"Ask Rosie, she would love to join you in the psychic stuff, maybe get all the *Charmed* together too. Strength in numbers. Don't worry, I will be back on Sunday, but you know, I think you'll have this all wrapped up by then."

"Thanks for the vote of confidence and enjoy the rest of your week. And, Sis, if you do find a good moment —"

"I'll ask him, I promise. Now, you said you still had to talk to that Wilson guy. Take care, okay?"

"Love you, Lady Lovington."

"The title suits me, right? Love you too. Give my regards to Auntie Pam."

***

My stomach was knotted all the way to Kenneth Wilson's cottage on the far side of the island. Dead Man's Cove was not as gothic as its name suggests, in fact, it is a pretty hamlet with over a dozen fisherman's cottages. The name derives from its history of smuggling. This small inlet was alive with entrepreneurs of opportunity back in the eighteenth century.

Unlike the Cornish coast and infamous smugglers of old, the authorities on Wesberrey at the time turned a blind eye to the locals' extra-curricular activities. Rumours survive to this day of hoards of rum and other exotic goods being hidden in the rock caves that make up this end of the island. The coastguard is often called out to rescue adventurous treasure hunters who get caught out in the tides. Hence the nefarious name.

The cottage was a single storey dwelling. White-washed against the elements, its wooden door and window frames bleached by the sun and sea. In the front, a small yard provided space for a rusty bicycle frame that rested humbly in the shadow of its shiny modern replacement.

With all the tales I had heard of Mr Wilson, I expected him to be an evasive character, but when I knocked on his front door, the string-thin octogenarian greeted me with a cheeky smile and a twinkle in his eye.

"Reverend Ward, I presume. I was expecting you. We need to figure out who framed your uncle."

Bessie

No commemorative plates or homespun artwork here. The living room snuggled around a large inglenook fireplace, its bricks blackened with centuries of use. To the side, a table with a digital replica of an art deco wooden radio played the greatest hits of ole blue eyes himself, Frank Sinatra.

"Do you want me to turn it off?" Ken Wilson plumped up a cushion on the fireside chair.

"No, I love the oldies."

"You can't beat a bit of Frank, eh?" He took his seat in the chair opposite me. "It's a snazzy device this. Connects to my phone and plays my favourites, like I have my own radio station."

"It looks authentic too." I scanned the room for further clues to his personality.

"Oh, I don't shy away from technological advances, but there's no need to throw the baby out with the bathwater, as they say. Modern designs don't have warmth or character. So, Reverend, we have ourselves a little predicament here, now don't we?"

"Have the police been around to talk to you?" I asked.

"No, not yet. But I got a call from that buffoon, Taylor, asking if I would be in this afternoon. I think he is doing all the donkey work."

"I've already met the other members of your squad. The police hadn't interviewed them either. In fact, neither of them knew my uncle had been arrested."

"Hmm, interesting." Ken jumped from his seat, his spindly legs finding shaky purchase on the rug before him. "Reverend, where are my manners? Would you like a cup of tea? Please don't refuse. I'm gasping myself. Need to keep hydrated, very important."

"Then if you insist, milk no sugar, thank you."

Ken's hunched bony frame doddered next door, giving me a chance to look around. Despite his age, and obvious frailty, he was nimble once he got moving. I would need to be quick.

The beamed walls and low ceiling were dust-free and un-ornamented. Old vinyl records stood crammed vertically into an oak cabinet. On the top were a few family photographs in silver and gold-plated frames. There was only one picture on the wall. One I knew well from my childhood of a Victorian girl crying against a wall, being watched by her faithful dog, a doll in a blue satin dress by her feet. I always wondered what the appeal of this print was. It's a sad image.

Ken's metal detector was by the front door. I didn't see it when I entered, because the door hid the device as I walked through.

So far, Kenneth Wilson was not as I had expected. He seemed a kind, old man. A bit of a loner, perhaps. Lonely even. He may have been a wise guy in his youth, but age punctures all our balloons. Would be intriguing to find out how he ended up as an accountant.

"Here we are, Reverend. Ah, I see you have found Bessie."

"Bessie?"

"Yes, isn't she a beauty?"

Ken placed our mugs on the coffee table in front of the fire and came to show me what Bessie could do.

"Had her for years now. They keep bringing out new models, you know. Deeper ground penetration. Linked to computers for soil and terrain analysis. But Bessie here does everything I need."

"Have you found anything really valuable?"

"Depends what you classify as valuable. I have found coins, of course, and a couple of brooches. Remains of weapons, sword hilts, etcetera, but not a full one, yet. That's my goal. We've had Roman and Viking invasions off this coast and all the wrecks over the years. It will amaze you what washes up. Find me a complete Viking sword and I shall die a happy man."

"I understand Greg Moorfield found something valuable earlier that morning. Do you know where it is now?"

Ken edged his way back to his chair. He collected his mug on the way, taking a sip before answering. "The ambergris? I imagine wherever he hid it. He was planning a treasure hunt. The winner takes all. Very generous of him, I mean, it was his find."

"Do you think that's what got him killed?"

"Why would anyone do that? They still stood a chance of winning it fair and square. Maybe they would kill the victor then, but it seems a tad premature to knock off poor Greg when he was being so accommodating."

I picked up my mug and settled in for further questions. "I hope you don't mind me asking, but all three of you are convinced my uncle is innocent. Do you have any suspicions about who did it?"

"Hmm," he leant back in the armchair and surveyed the Artex on the ceiling for inspiration. "How do you know it's one of us? Okay, they killed him outside our hut, but that's a public beach. Could've been anyone."

"How would anyone have used Byron's nail gun? They must have gotten that from the hut."

"I guess, though it's common knowledge Byron never locks the shed at the end of his garden. There's a path that runs along the back. Wouldn't be any trouble to jump over the low hedge and steal it away. If he hadn't lent it out to them already. He was always loaning out his tools."

"When you say common knowledge, how common?"

"Well, we all knew. I would borrow tools all the time. The others too. In fact, I think Meacham has had his sander for over a year!" Ken chuckled to himself, spilling some of his tea over the edge of the mug. "Ah, look at me! Such a mess."

"So Byron was a trusting soul. He is a good man."

"Well, he's your uncle. Don't you know? None of it makes any sense. Now if you told me it was hoity-toity Cummings or pass-me-a-spliff Meacham, I would be less shocked. Surprised, maybe. But Byron? I'm gob-smacked. Whoever did this terrible thing picked the wrong fall guy. Or maybe that's the point. It's always the quiet ones."

I felt as if we were going around in endless circles, each member of the beach squad suggesting the other, but none believing it was my uncle.

"Mr Wilson. I don't know all the details. It's very frustrating, but I believe someone discovered Greg Moorfield's body the night he died. Or that there was even a witness. Do you know if that's correct?"

"No, not at all. I mean, I don't know." Ken knocked back the last dregs of his tea. "All I know is, we all met outside his house for the treasure hunt and he wasn't at home. The dog was there. Howling for its supper, poor thing."

"So? What did you do? Report his disappearance to PC Taylor? Go searching for him?"

"It was dark, and to be honest, we were there because he had gone to so much effort. And, well... lonely old men wandering the streets on Halloween isn't a welcome sight. The world is very distrustful these days, don't you find?"

Ken fiddled with the cushion behind his back.

"And?"

"And what? Oh, right, we all went home," he replied.

Really?

"Without checking everything was okay?"

"Well, obviously, with hindsight, we should have put together a search party or something. But, it's easy to be wise after the fact, isn't it? There was nothing to indicate there was any trouble." Ken peered into his mug, his face disappointed at the emptiness within. "The old duffer could have fallen asleep. I can be dead to the world. Nothing wakes me up. There was this time when I was in Istanbul, huge earthquake, buildings collapsing all around me and I slept through the lot!"

Ken twisted his wrist, still holding the mug, to check his watch, then inched forward to the edge of his chair.

"Well, Reverend, it's been an absolute delight meeting you. We should do it again someday. I'm sure you're a busy lady, with a thousand and one things to do today."

"True, but my uncle is my priority."

"Of course, of course. Family is so important." He placed the mug carefully on the coffee table. "And I wouldn't trust the boys in blue not to stitch up Byron like a kipper.

In my experience, the Old Bill looks for quick wins. If you present them with a gift suspect, wrapped up in a bow, they're delighted."

"So you think someone framed my uncle? Do you know who?"

"Of course he's being framed, but I have no idea who or why. To be honest, I can't see why anyone would want to harm Moorfield either. What did that old fool ever do to anyone? Now, shooting Cummings between the eyes, that I would understand."

Ken laughed to himself as he pressed down on the arms of his chair to raise himself up. "Now, if you'll excuse me, Reverend, it's time for my meds. Not a pretty sight, so I'm afraid I have to ask you to leave."

We'll Meet Again

I left Cilla outside Mr Wilson's cottage and took a stroll along the beach. Nothing about this scenario made sense, and I needed a consultation with the Big Guy upstairs. I found a comfy-looking rock and climbed atop to listen to the sea. The waves breathed in and out, their watery drum roll keeping rhythm with all that is and ever was.

There are numerous scientific studies showing the benefits of living by the sea. The negative ions increase serotonin levels, increasing our general levels of happiness, and the minerals and vitamins in the water help prevent physical and mental ill-health. Saltwater is great for curing skin conditions, such as eczema. Some reports state that there is a decrease in cases of lung cancer. Taking a daily swim offsets dementia. And wave-watching relieves anxiety and depression.

I paused for several minutes, just to drink in the splendour of the vista before me. To relish the evidence of God's bounty on my horizon, meditate on this case and what we have discovered so far.

Except, I had nothing. No clues, just riddles. Whilst all agreed my uncle was an unlikely murderer and Greg Moorfield an equally unlikely victim, he was very dead and my uncle was very much in the frame.

The waves crashed against the smaller rocks in front. The tide was coming in. A billowy lace skirt played kiss chase with the surf as it returned to the sea. I watched the foam slink back, only to be caught out by the next approaching wave.

In the rock pools that remained and out in the wide ocean beyond, life struggled in its daily quest to survive. Death, or the threat of death, is a constant presence. Ashes to ashes, dust to dust.

That phrase always challenged me. My church teaches life everlasting and yet, at the end, we talk of our temporal truth in the starkest of terms. Our prayers hope for the life hereafter. We beg our Heavenly Father to accept our departed loved one into his home.

I have questioned how a lovely parent could turn his children away when the alternative is an eternity in the blazing fires of hell. Now, my recent experiences suggest we all transcend to the light. No judgement, just a loving embrace. *Isn't that what any father would do?*

When I cross over, I expect my father to be waiting for me. That the years and the pain will melt away. All blame and bitterness are cast aside in the true light of forgiveness. If that is not to be, what is the point of it all?

I pulled my coat tight. The autumn air whipped around the headland and pulled my gaze to the surrounding rocks. It was easy to picture stranded wrecks of yesteryear bashed against this craggy coast. The automated lighthouse, a hundred yards away, still warned ships of the danger. So few vessels come close enough to this stretch of the shore these days to warrant employing a full-time keeper on this side of the island.

It would be easy to smuggle through this beach. No patrols, no coastguard on site. It will be pitch dark after sunset.

Maybe the ambergris is a red herring? What if this is all a smokescreen to hide an international drugs ring shipping their goods into England through the sleepy Isle of Wesberrey?

I felt myself spinning, not with nausea or dizziness, but with a dark melancholy. From all accounts, Greg Moorfield was a good man with no natural enemies. My uncle, the same. Neither appeared to have an evil bone in their bodies and yet here I was gazing out across the ocean, failing miserably to find either motives or insights that would solve the death of the former and exonerate the latter. *Except for a ridiculous plotline of smugglers and whale vomit thieves that even the combined talents of Robert De Niro and Al Pacino would struggle to pull off convincingly.*

I had asked the Boss for help already. I hate to pester him with my petty grievances. He is so busy. *But I really need his help, like, yesterday. Deep breath and focus.*

The wind caught a tear from my eye and whisked it away into the incoming spray. Water licked at my shoes.

I should probably head back.

Just a few more minutes. The lines to heaven must be busy.

The tide receded. Time for another speedy intercession. *Note to self: Make it clear, this time, how serious I am about needing his assistance.*

Heavenly Father, you know I don't ask for much. I have all that I need. I have my faith, my health, my family and friends, and I have Lawrence. I am incredibly blessed and want for nothing, through your grace. But, right now, I need your help to prove my uncle's innocence and find out who killed Greg Moorfield. You have decided, in your all-powerful wisdom, to give me these abilities. Show me how I can use them for the benefit of others. Help me reconcile my faith and my gifts so that I may be a more effective instrument of your love. Thank you.

I waited for the peace to flow through me.

The desire to know the serenity and comfort of God's infinite wisdom filled every cell.

I listened for inspiration, but only heard the gulls squawking overhead and distant calls of panic and fear.

"Reverend! Oi! Come back in. The tide will take you!"

Not before I get an answer...

"Reverend Ward!"

Just a little longer...

Cold plumes of water lashed my ankles. The foamy remains of the tide swirled around the base of the rock. I had to go. Turning to retrace my path, I found it had all but vanished. A few peaks made guest appearances above the surface of the waves, receding from view as the tide gained momentum.

"Oh, blast!"

Jess, you're a complete fool. What are you going to do now, eh? Swim for it?

I stood up, panic-stricken. Fear gluing my feet firm. I turned to see who had been calling my name, but no one was in sight.

Great! Some psychic you are, couldn't even predict the tide would come in.

"Here, Reverend! Grab the end of this."

Kenneth Wilson pushed a long wooden pole towards me. It was a good five yards long. He hunkered down behind a grass mound, feeding out the pike.

After several feeble attempts, I caught hold, and he squatted hard and walked slowly backwards.

My imagination flooded with images of my rescuer flying into the air if I put too much weight on my end, but he was stronger than his frail body suggested and soon I was scrabbling up the bank. Wetter, but wiser.

"Thank you so much, Mr Wilson. I lost complete track of time. I am so sorry. That was too stupid for words. I risked both our lives."

Ken raised the pike to his side. It towered over us both.

"Good thing I had Henry Pikestaff here. Took a while to get him down from the beam. I'm not as spritely as I once was."

"Do you name all your inanimate belongings?" I snickered, more out of embarrassment than snooty ridicule. "I am very grateful for the services of Henry Pikestaff.

"He's a true gentleman. Let's go back inside and warm you by the fire."

Hi-De-Hi

My sodden socks looked lonely on the top rung of the wooden rack. The expandable airer somehow consumed all the heat from the fireplace. The socks were toasty warm, yet I was turning to ice. I wasn't ungrateful, though, for the chance to drip dry.

"Are you sure you don't want me to add your trousers as well? The clothes horse here has plenty of room."

"No, I'm fine, Mr Wilson. Thank you."

I am not sitting here with a potential killer half-naked. Even if that same suspect saved my life.

"Suit yourself, Reverend. No need to be shy. I've seen legs before. After National Service, I got a job at Butlin's, you know, the holiday camp. Hi-De-HI!

A faint memory of enforced entertainment and communal games amidst concrete housing blocks and neat lawn gardens flashed before my eyes.

"I think Mum took us to one once. Skegness?""Yes, that's where I worked, the first camp in Britain, and the best, in my humble opinion. Great times." A faraway mist tinged his elderly eyes as he reminisced about the past. "Anyway, it was my pleasure to judge the Lovely Legs and the Knobbly Knees competitions for three years straight. Every week, once a week, all summer long. Lower limbs hold no mystery for me now."

"I dare say. But I'm comfortable here. Only the hems are damp, the rest of me is fine."

Ken shifted the drying rack a few degrees to reach his chair and sat down. "I have to ask, what were you doing out there?"

"Thinking," I grinned.

"About what? You were away with the fairies. I fetched Henry Pikestaff to poke you awake and just as well I did. A few more seconds and you'd have been crab food."

"I have to say I was impressed with how you wielded that weapon. It must weigh a ton."

Ken puffed himself up in the chair. "Strong upper arms courtesy of a wasted youth spent as an amateur pugilist. Bantamweight. Only thing I took from two darn years pounding concrete for Queen and country. Could have turned professional, but I fell for the charms of a pretty lady from Knightsbridge who was dead against me doing anything that could spoil my boyish good looks."

"You gave up your career for love, that is very romantic."

I wanted to draw him out. I had a second chance at this conversation and empathy is the best way to gain trust.

"Oh, no. Quite the opposite. She ran a club in the West End and wanted her security team to look like Hollywood movie stars. It was the sixties, and I was in the heart of London life. I met Princess Margaret, Oliver Reed was a regular, and there was always a buzz when the Krays paid a visit."

I think you would have got on a riot with my Aunt Cindy.

"Sounds exciting."

"Well, Reverend, it was a lot better than donkey derbies and weekly tombolas. A fitted Italian suit trumps a Red Coat any day."

Interesting as this exchange was, it told me little more than that the frail old man who sat beside me had been a vigorous youth, though I understood how others had seen him as a bit of a wise guy. Not everyone can claim to have known Ronnie and Reggie Kray, the East End's most famous gangsters.

"Mr Wilson, you seem a good judge of character. All your years in security must have taught you a few things about people. Who would you put your money on for Greg Moorfield's murder?"

"As a former accountant, well..." He leaned forward and cupped his mouth to whisper, "actually I was a bookmaker, don't tell anyone." He clicked his tongue and placed a knowing finger to the side of his nose. "Doesn't have the same kudos, if you get me drift. Out of Paul and Roger? I'd put twenty pounds on each."

***

Clothes dry and dignity semi-preserved, I bid my goodbyes and took Cilla to Pamela's house. I hoped to find out more about my uncle and why anyone would want to frame him for murder. On the way, I prayed she would be alone. I suspected that having Cindy or my mother present would hamper the conversation.

The sepia memories of my childhood are littered with animated conversations the *Charmed* sisterhood had about their husbands or significant others. Cindy, in particular, enjoyed taking the rise out of her older sibling for settling down with someone so vanilla. I used to pretend to be absorbed in a book or magazine when I eavesdropped. They would have said nothing if they thought I was listening.

This echo from my past suggested that Aunt Pamela would talk more freely if her sisters weren't there. Regardless, it was nearly two in the afternoon, and I was starving. If I couldn't get answers, I could at least get fed.

Pamela was standing on the porch when I pulled up outside.

I released the jaw strap of my scooter helmet and crunched my way up the path. "How did you know I was coming?"

"I should say I saw your arrival in my crystal ball, but actually I was sweeping the front step, the leaves had blown in. Usually, Byron sees to it, but —"

I went in for a hug.

My family is not very tactile. Mum flinches at the slightest hint of an emotional display. But my less stoic aunt needed propping up. We held each other beyond the British standard measure for acceptable physical contact outside a front door, which at its best is normally an air kiss on the cheek and a wave in passing.

"Is there anyone else inside?"

"No, just me. I know they mean well, but they were driving me insane." A wry smile followed. "There are good reasons siblings usually go their separate ways on reaching adulthood. I have made us some lunch."

"So you did know I was coming!" I followed my aunt into the hall and held back to hang my coat on the stand.

She smirked back over her shoulder. "Of course. I really hope you will stick around this afternoon, we have a lot of work to do."

***

Pamela's premonitory and culinary abilities had produced a hearty beef stew swimming with carrots, leeks and fluffy dumpling islands.

I apologise to the animals who were sacrificed for this offering to the gods of taste, but this is a worthy tribute.

"You'll have to teach me how to do this." I harpooned a mushroom trapped beneath a meat chunk.

"The stew or the psychic intuition?"

"Both."

My aunts were so comfortable with their powers. They had been aware of their abilities from birth. Mum had shielded her daughters from this knowledge. I understood her reasons, but now we were playing catch up. For my sisters, it was a fun hobby, like discovering you can paint watercolours, but for me, there was a role to be played and I still knew nothing about what the expectations of the job were, nor how I would attempt to fulfil them.

"Well, I can give you the recipe for the stew. Rosie can make a vegan version, I'm sure. I felt you needed meat. As to the rest..." My aunt balanced her fork on the edge of her bowl and linked her fingers together.

There was a pause.

"I think I need to show you."

A Quiet Afternoon

Dishes rinsed in the sink, Pam suggested we sit on the floor of her lounge. Backs against the floral sofas for support, our bodies eased themselves into position to a symphony of puffs and grunts.

"There was a time I could sit cross-legged without snapping my knees in two." Pam leant on me for support as she adjusted her position. "Cindy still can, of course. But then Cindy can do anything."

There was always a barb to my oldest aunt's comments about her youngest sibling's talents or lifestyle. Pam had believed that she was to be the Godmother, the great protector of the triple wells. Her dream came crashing down when she fell pregnant. It was the sixties, and she and Byron did the honourable thing and married. Though their marriage had lasted nearly sixty years, it must hurt to see your baby sister living the life you had so passionately desired.

Was she jealous? Maybe, though I struggled to see what there was to be envious about. Cindy may still turn somersaults in her yoga practice and heads when she enters a room, but what else did being the Godmother add to her life? She was alone, childless, and now her powers were fading.

"Aunt Pamela, maybe this isn't the right time to ask, but I still don't really understand what you expect of me as the Godmother. I'm not prepared for whatever it is. My uncle needs my help so badly and yet, I have discovered nothing. What good am I?"

"Why do you think we are on the floor? Just hold my hand and empty your mind of all this chatter."

Taking Pam's hand was the easy bit. She tetched beside me as I struggled to clear away my thoughts.

"It's like Grand Central Station up there," she giggled. "Not that I've ever been to New York, or the USA, for that matter. No small wonder you are failing to grasp what's going on. Too much traffic. How can you hear the spirit if you are making so much noise?"

"I hear my God," I protested, flinching at her tightening grip.

"Really? Well, let's hope he's trying to get through. We need all the help we can get."

My aunt was enjoying this, I could sense it. Her husband was rotting away in a prison cell on the mainland, and yet this latest dose of magic was firing her up. I could feel a lifetime's longing to practice her conjuring gifts bubbling inside me like magma. We were one, and her distant yearning for opportunities past rose in my chest. A tear escaped. I turned to see if she was crying too.

"Don't feel sorry for things that were not to be," she whispered. "It is your time now."

My tongue stuck fast against my upper palate. A creamy sensation filled my throat. Unlike before, there was no nausea, simply a strong desire to yawn. My jaw widened but there was no sound. I was mute. Gagged. Silenced.

"Open your eyes."

I hadn't realised they were closed.

"Whaaat the —"

There was no ground beneath us, only darkness and streaking lights passing around us as we plummeted downwards.

Has Pam slipped me some LSD?

"I can hear your thoughts."

Of course, you can, silly me.

"You aren't silly. Relax"

Stop thinking. Stop thinking. Stop thinking.

"That would be very helpful, thank you."

Aargh!

"You can't help yourself, can you?" Pamela shouted over the whooshing airstream sucking us down. "Buckle up, we're nearly there. Get ready, it can be quite the bump."

I didn't realise my aunt had such a sarcastic sense of humour.

We landed. Not so much as with a whimper, but a bang.

"Where are we?" I scanned the horizon. It was eerily familiar.

"Wesberrey, of course. The correct question is when are we."

I scrambled my battered body upright and stood to take in the world around me. To my left, shadow figures processed to a round stone structure. Behind us, the land sloped down to a grassy plain and then dropped again towards a cliff edge. Sounds of the sea beyond played hidden beneath a rolling mist carpet. The sun hung low in the sky, casting all before it with a rose-gold hue.

"I know this place."

I stumbled forward, the uncultivated land lay soft beneath my feet. The wild grass remained damp from an earlier

163

shower. Unmanicured. Untamed. A bramble caught at my trouser giving the nettle beside it a window to bite my ankle.

"Ouch!" I bent down to rub where it stung. "That was a little too realistic."

My aunt crouched beside me. "Allow me." She waved a hand over the offending wound and it warmed under her touch. "You still don't understand. Listen to the spirit that runs through every cell of your being. All this is as real as the stones in the walls of your beloved St. Bridget's"

"Okay, so who are they then?" I gestured to the shadow folk now chanting rhymes in a circle.

"You really do not know? Breathe in the air. Feel your destiny." Pam straightened up and laced her arm around my waist. "Come, let's introduce you."

The group parted as we drew near. The stone wall was a well. Corn dollies, pebbles, shells and sprigs of herbs decorated the top.

"This is the well in your garden!"

"Yes, my dear." Pam pivoted me around to face the circle. "And these are your predecessors. Say hello to your ancestors."

Grey sunken eyes obviously run in the family.

Pam glared. I forgot she could read my thoughts.

I managed an embarrassed smirk.

"Jessamy, my little pudding. Come, it's been too long."

One of the skeletal figures stepped towards me, arms outstretched. The closer she came, the more fleshed out her features became.

"Grandma?"

My grandmother turned to the others, her pride a halo of light that illuminated all their faces. I recognised my great-grandmother, only from old family photo albums. The rest were strangers, to me, at any rate. They all knew who I was and surged forward to join in our embrace.

My grandmother turned and beat them back.

"One at a time, don't overwhelm the poor child. Pammie, my love. Thank you so much for bringing her to visit. It has been too long. Jessamy is a grown woman!"

Pam kissed her mother on the cheek, and the love rolled down her face in liquid crystal droplets.

"Beverley took them away, remember? Jess knows nothing."

My grandmother tutted and shook her head. "I blame that wretch she married. Beverley should have stayed. We were there for her. For all of you."

She clapped her hands and circular mounds rose from the grass, creating seats soon filled with the other godmothers and their sisters. One I recognised as my great-aunt – Cindy's predecessor. In the centre, a fire blazed. They invited me to sit down.

Pam nudged me. "The fire is just for show. They can't feel hot or cold."

My grandmother continued her tirade against my father. She remained a formidable woman, even in the next world (or wherever we were.)

"And where is Cynthia? This is her job to do."

"I don't think she's well enough to travel." Pam squeezed my hand. More to comfort herself than me. In that instant, I knew it wasn't only Cindy's powers that were fading, but also her temporal light.

My grandmother took a pragmatic breath. "Then you did the right thing, Pammie, dear."

The circle fell silent. There was a gap in the centre.

"Who are we waiting for?"

"Briganti, the High One."

"The Goddess herself?" I gasped.

A trumpet sounded, and everyone rose.

The Goddess

Briganti's face shimmered. Her gossamer hair changed colour with every inward breath. Pale to dark. Golden, red and brown. Her translucent skin pulsed cream through to ebony and back again. Her eyes, too, flickered through a rainbow of hues. She was mesmerising. Luminescent. Hypnotic.

"Welcome, Beloved."

My heart lightened hearing her ethereal voice. Joy swelled in my chest, and my flesh tingled.

"Jessamy, sweet child of love, a beautiful name. I called you after the jasmine flower. So delicate and fragrant, yet tenacious and resilient. It suits you well."

Excitement ran over me. I wanted to squeal. Obviously, I was on some acid trip, though the sting in my ankle had left a physical mark. I would awaken soon. For now, however, my stomach somersaulted as if I was meeting all my teenage heroes at once. Teenage heroes, I didn't know I had.

This can't be happening.

Pam squeezed my hand. "It is real. Accept it. Your spirit knows. Listen to your heart. You are our guest of honour. The Goddess is here to show you the truth."

Silly mind-melting trick. Can't a girl think in peace?

"My child," Briganti glowed a freckled bronze with platinum white hair. "Ask whatever questions you have."

All eyes were upon me.

It may be a dream, but I needed answers to so many questions.

"I am an Anglican priest. I have my own faith. I believe in one true God. How am I supposed to believe in you as well?"

"You do not need to believe, just know."

Ah, my aunts' propensity for riddles has a long lineage.

"Okay, well, and how do I fit into all this?"

The Goddess, now glistening a burnished copper with coal-black tresses, beamed a look familiar to any child who's tried to argue with their mother for more pieces of birthday cake. That knowing tell that says you've already tucked away four slices, but I'll play along (in time, you will understand why I was going to say no).

"My child. You are the One. You protect the portal."

"The portal?"

Pam nudged my arm with her elbow. "The wells. All three are gateways for the Goddess to cross."

"Even the one under my church font? She won't get far if she tries to get through that."

My ghostly ancestors centred their collective gaze upon me. I don't think they appreciated my sense of humour.

Unphased, with skin like mahogany and dazzling violet eyes, Briganti continued.

"We travel through water and air. The water cleanses us before we return from your world. To bring harmony and peace, we swim with the dolphins and soar with the eagles. We watch over the faithful and shepherd the weak." Her presence grew stronger with every word, forming a halo around her. "Your faith helps restore balance because it is pure. Not everyone's beliefs encourage love. Many bring hate and greed. They are destroying the veil, allowing pain and suffering where there should be joy. The joy you feel in your heart right now."

"So my job is to look after a well?"

That should be easy enough. Not sure I need magic powers to do that, though.

"They are not magic powers." Briganti glowered.

Of course, the Goddess can hear my thoughts too.

"Everyone on earth can do what you can do. It is your job to remind them. To move them from faith to knowing. From believing in a higher power to experiencing it."

"Not everyone can speak to the dead," I exclaimed. "Not everyone can relive past events by holding something related in their hands."

"Exactly," she applauded. "You understand."

No, I don't.

The Goddess tilted her head. Her lips curled. *There's that enigmatic smile again.*

"And God? What about him?"

"There is no God. There is no Goddess. There is all." Briganti lifted her palms skyward and raised her voice. "I am the manifestation of love. So is the Heavenly Father you worship. Though there is no need to worship him. You need only to know he is with you and he is the truth. Knowing him. Knowing me. Understanding this is all that is. Embracing that truth is the way. Love binds us together. It matters not how you choose to see that love, as long as you know it in your heart."

"So, you're saying everything I believed until now is false?"

"No, you are saying that."

"No, I'm not. I am sure of my faith."

I am, aren't I?

Pam patted my hand. "Please, let go and listen. Don't filter, just hear the message."

"So, I don't need to pray to you. Or bow down before you. Or live my life following your commandments?"

Briganti's turquoise eyes twinkled. "We have no need of your supplication. We are all that is. We are Alpha and Omega, the beginning and the end. We are the Word. We are the Light."

"You and God are one."

"No, my dear. We are all one."

"Then why does my family have to offer a daughter each generation to be your protector?"

"True love is sacrifice. Buddha resisted temptation and meditated away from the world to reach Nirvana. Mohammad received the Quran whilst sitting quietly in a cave. Jesus actually died on the cross. They had to give up their lives to teach others the truth."

"But they created world religions. I would be the god-mother for a handful of people by comparison."

"No, my child. You are a vessel. Your presence allows wisdom to flow. You will know what we require when it is time."

"And my current job?"

"You will find, my child, they are one and the same."

***

Time up. My audience over, Briganti rose and crossed the circle to kiss me on both cheeks. Then she faded away. No fireworks, no fanfare. She evaporated. My predecessors followed one by one until only my grandmother and great-grandmother remained.

Grandma cupped my face in both her hands. "You wanted to know, and now you know. You must find your way to serve. Like my sweet Pammie here, I used herbs and potions. Cindy takes after my sister and works with her own energy. You will find your way, but first, you must open your heart and mind. Let your soul guide you."

I kissed her palm, and she turned to say farewell to my aunt.

"Pammie, my sweetest daughter, do not worry about Cindy. She has worked hard to fight the evils of this modern world. She needs a rest, don't you think?"

My aunt nodded. "And Beverley? At least she is back home."

Grandma looked at her mother, and they smiled in unison. "You will have each other when Cindy is gone."

Pam pulled her mother close for a final embrace, and then they left.

No drama, no puffs of smoke or screeching owls. They faded away like the rest.

The land beneath us rumbled. The wind curled at our feet. Pamela took my hand and once again, I was pushing back the solid mass in my mouth. Falling at speed towards my aunt's Wilton carpet.

After a breathless beat to let the rest of my torso catch up with my rear end, I squared up to Pam to demand more answers.

"Is Cindy dying?"

"She is unwell. Yes." Pam swung her legs under her as she used the sofa to lift herself up.

With less grace, I followed her example. "But she seems so healthy. Does Mum know?"

"Of course. We can all sense each other's life force. Don't you feel the same connection with your sisters?"

We are very close, even more so since returning to the island, but we were siblings. It's normal.

"Aunt Pam, aren't you worried?"

Her dark brown eyes penetrated deep into my psyche. It was like I could physically feel her rooting around for the key to unlock my stupidity.

"I will miss her," she replied.

"That's not the same thing."

"No, it's not. But it is the most honest answer I can give you. I am worried about myself. I worry for those she will leave behind, who will mourn her in the belief that they will never see her again. But I know I will. Isn't that a great comfort to the soul? That is our mission. That's your job."

I wanted to understand. I really did.

"What if I refuse to be the next goddess protector? Cindy will stay here then, right?"

Pam shook her hand. "We all have our allotted hour." She reached across and took my hands. "You cannot change what they have ordained. But you can help those here that need your assistance, like my sweet Byron."

"Aunt Pam, I would love to. I just don't know how."

***

Astral jaunting, or whatever it was we had just done, takes a lot of energy. Pam advised me to refuel with several sugary snacks over the next few hours and stuffed a bunch of Twix chocolate bars into Cilla's saddlebags before I left.

I flipped up the kickstand and walked my scooter towards Buck's house. My mind was too unsteady to be in charge of driving a motorised vehicle. I still wasn't sure what I had experienced. A shared hallucination, perhaps like mass hysteria, except there were only two of us. Or perhaps I was in a hypnotic trance.

My ankle still smarted, but that could have been part of the deception. Stinging nettles collected from my aunt's garden in advance, or possibly already lying around for some witchy potion or simple nettle tea.

Why do you doubt what you have seen with your own eyes?

I turned to see who was talking.

There was no one there.

I am with you as you are with me.

It was Briganti.

"Uh-huh. Who do you think I am, Joan of Arc? Get out of my head. Now!"

I was screaming at myself in the middle of the street. Fortunately, there was still no one around.

I will be here whenever you need me.

"Good to know. Now, can you leave me alone?"

I paused and waited for a ghostly reply.

Note to self: remember to buy a poppy from the British Legion stall in Market Square tomorrow.

Silence.

I had never been so relieved to have a mundane, actionable thought.

***

There's a low wall at the corner of Buck's estate. I parked Cilla, grabbed a Twix bar and sat on the brick edge for about ten minutes in quiet-ish contemplation.

The sun had set, and house lights twinkled below. Each light a home or business where people were going about their evening routine. Normal lives led by ordinary people. Some with faith, others non-believers. All of them were blissfully unaware of the knowledge I had. The insight into the life hereafter I couldn't give them. Not that they would believe me. I didn't believe it myself.

I bit at the serrated corner of the gold chocolate wrapper and carelessly spat the corner out. It landed in the gutter. A rivulet of water carried it downhill to the main drain grate.

It must be raining.

I hadn't noticed.

I pushed the chocolate and caramel covered stick of shortbread up from its snug casing and took a large bite.

My aunt was going to die. She had used up all her energy. Without her abilities, there was no need to continue. Is that what happens to us all? We come here for a purpose and once that task is done, we return home.

There should be something comforting in that knowledge, that no life is wasted, no matter how short, and we are all here to fulfil a higher truth. That there is a plan. We all have a destiny. That we live forever and are one.

I wanted to believe. I wanted to find peace with this. It was, after all, the very cornerstone of my religion. And yet… I was unworthy. Too fragile. Too scared.

The last piece of chocolate stopped the screams from my mouth. The rain drowned out my tears.

I may never have peace again. I found no solace in knowing the truth, even if it was the truth. It shattered my foundations like a car windscreen after a collision. Seemingly intact, but loosely held in a million pieces. One knock and it would all come apart.

Jess, sort yourself out! This is ridiculous. So, either you are losing your mind or you found out God is real, just not how you imagined. Grow up! Byron needs you to pull it together. People are depending on you. You can throw a self-pity party later on.

I scrunched the gold wrapper into my pocket. Took a deep breath and told Cilla we had to go on a few more yards.

Nothing crazy about talking to a hunk of metal, right?

Mind Games

T illy greeted me at the front door. "You look like a drowned raccoon."

Note to self: buy waterproof mascara.

"Why were you pushing your scooter?"

I unwrapped myself from my soaking wet clothes. This was the second time today I was stripping off wet layers in someone else's house.

"Long story. Is everyone here?"

"Yeah, in the kitchen." Tilly skipped down the hall. "Dad, the reverend needs some dry clothes. Can I borrow your clean sweats?"

Buck yelled back his agreement and Tilly rushed back to lead me upstairs. She opened a cupboard on the landing and grabbed some towels.

"Wait here a sec. I will get you something to wear. I would offer you something of mine but..."

She eyed me up and down. I got her drift immediately.

"No worries. I doubt your trousers would get past my thunder thighs."

Or even past my swollen ankles!

Seconds later, I was drying off in the bathroom, admiring the blue and white nautical theme. They had framed the circular mirror above the sink like a porthole on a ship, and there was even a model yacht on the windowsill.

Fortunately for me, Buck was a big hulk of a man, and his sweatpants had a working drawstring at the waist. I rolled up the arm and ankle cuffs and headed downstairs. Rosie was waiting for me at the bottom.

"Jess, what's the matter? Tilly said you were soaked to the skin. She thought you had been crying."

I put a comforting hand on my baby sister's shoulder and tried to make eye contact, but couldn't hold it for long. Water pressed against my eyeballs. I tilted my head from side to side to shake the tears away.

"I'll tell you later. Has Buck filled you all in on what we found this morning?"

And it was only that morning that we discovered the metal chest, though it felt like a lifetime ago.

Rosie nodded. She linked her arm through mine as we walked to the kitchen. Lawrence, Buck, and Luke were talking tactics in the corner as Tilly played with photographs on the table. Alfie greeted me with an exuberant wagging of his tail before continuing on his quest to claim the sofa in the lounge.

"Luke has been busy." Tilly beamed. "We have pictures of all the suspects."

My nephew broke away from the huddle of testosterone and joined us at the table. Hands deep in his black jean pockets, he shuffled up next to his beau.

"I didn't get too close but zoomed in as best I could."

The pictures showed all three men outside the beach hut.

"Luke, when did you take these?"

"On the way here. I thought I should get some of the crime scene, and they were all outside talking."

"Did you hear what they were talking about?"

"No, like I said, I didn't want to get too close. I pretended I was taking selfies." He blew some wisps of his wavy fringe from his eyes. "They didn't suspect a thing. So, which one's which?"

Tilly rested her head on his shoulder. Their curls intertwined until it was hard to tell where Tilly ended and Luke began. *They would make beautiful squiggly haired babies.*

I crossed the room to get a clearer look and pointed the suspects out, taking a few minutes to recap what I had spoken about with each one. As I talked, Lawrence slid behind me and wrapped his arms around my waist. Buck took note and mirrored this public display of affection with my sister on the other side of the table.

There was so much love in the room. I could feel the joy pulse through every cell of my being.

Love binds us together.

"Right!" I broke away from Lawrence and clapped to draw everyone's attention. "We need to go to Greg Moorfield's house and look for clues about the treasure hunt or his murderer. One will lead us to the other."

***

"What do we say if anyone sees us?" Rosie drew the curtains in Greg's lounge. "All the neighbours know the house is empty."

The torch on Buck's phone was already deep inside a cabinet drawer. "Dog treats, or toys. Say Alfie is pining or something."

Rosie danced across the carpet mimicking 'jazz hands'. "And the rubber gloves?"

"We're all a little OCD?" Tilly suggested.

"Or we didn't want to add our prints to a potential crime scene." Lawrence lifted a mirror from the wall above the fireplace. "We need to be systematic, quick and thorough."

"Remember, we are looking for treasure hunt clues or anything that points to a motive or one of the suspects." I patted down a cushion. "And keys. If we can locate the key to the chest, we don't need any more clues."

"Roger that." Lawrence slipped off the back of one of the picture frames that had stood on the mantelpiece. "Do we know if anyone has contacted his family yet?"

"The police would do that. But if we find an address book, we can send them our condolences."

The third cushion had a loose cover with a zip. On the front was a faux tapestry image of a country cottage. I opened it and pulled out the cotton-lined insert. I massaged the foam inner, but there was nothing of interest.

I flicked my hand around the inside of the cover and touched the end of a folded slip of paper in the corner.

"I've found something."

I moved towards the centre of the living room and unfolded the paper under the ceiling lamp.

"Well done. You found my little home. The next clue is a pile of bones."

Luke ran to the kitchen. "It must be with the dog food."

We all followed, getting jammed in the doorway as we watched him search. Buck squeezed through. "I may have taken the clue next door when I collected Alfie. Do you want me to check?"

Luke's black mop appeared over the door of the base unit. "No need, I've got it." He rose up with the paper in his hand. "Right. This one says. Another find, you are so kind. The next clue rests inside my mind."

"Darn it!" Buck kicked the oven. "So he's taken the next clue to the grave."

"Not necessarily." Lawrence pulled back into the lounge. "I think I know where it is. There's a phrenology head in the front room."

The lesser brains left behind looked at each other blankly and shrugged. As we walked through the door, Lawrence was proudly waving the third clue in his hand.

"You're nearly there. Oh, aren't you clever? The final clue is in the cellar."

"Well, that clue's just as dumb as dirt. There's no basement in these new builds."

Rosie kissed Buck on the cheek. "There's more than one kind of cellar, silly. Come, let me introduce you to the culinary arts."

Rosie led Buck by the hand back into the kitchen. On the worktop stood a vintage ceramic canister marked 'farine'. My sister took off the lid, and carefully emptied the contents, spreading the white flour with her fingers until they alighted upon a silver key.

"I found the precious." She whispered in a weak, raspy voice.

"Very funny, Sis." I held out my hand and nodded at her to drop the 'precious' onto my waiting palm.

Reluctant to hand over her prize, my sister paused. Buck stepped forward and guided Rosie to the table. "You should do it. You worked it out."

He's right. To the winner the spoils.

Rosie melted at his touch. A noticeable spark ran through her body. She giggled as she inserted the key into the lock and turned it. "High school French finally came in useful."

It fits.

A deep breath later, lid opened and smell unleashed; Rosie slammed it shut again. "That's the whale vomit alright. Man, that's ripe!"

Buck choked. "That stuff is worth thousands of dollars?"

"And worth taking someone's life for." I sighed. "But we are no closer to knowing who did it.

"No," Rosie handed me the locked box. "But we can take this to the police."

"Or better still," suggested Tilly, "We could use it as bait!"

White Flag

We agreed to discuss both options over an aubergine and split pea stew Rosie had warming in the oven next door. Lawrence and I stayed behind to lock up whilst the others got everything ready.

"Jess, I've been meaning to ask if you're okay, but with everyone there..."

No, I'm not okay. I met a goddess or dreamed I did. My aunt is going to die. 'All You Need Is Love'. The Beatles were right, go figure... And I'm quietly going mad!

"Thanks. I'm fine. Was just a little tired and wet, that's all."

Lawrence bent down to nuzzle the top of my head. "You would tell me, wouldn't you? No secrets, right?"

"No secrets. I promise."

Not a great start to our engagement. I was already holding back. I knew he would be gentle and understanding and probably extremely logical about what had taken place and how I should handle it. Lawrence embraced the witchy nonsense much better than I. But then it wasn't his gift that would kill off his aunt. It was mine.

I needed an excuse to break away from his compassionate inquisition.

"Let's just double-check that we've put everything back as we found it."

The cushions on the sofa were askew, so I adjusted them. The busyness was a useful distraction. I needed some more space before returning next door. The burden in my soul was weighty, and every polite word of conversation was tortuous.

Lawrence planted his lanky frame on the sofa, ruining my hard work. He patted the space beside him.

"Right. This won't do now, will it? In under two months, we are going to be married. And I don't know about you, but that's a solemn vow I plan to take seriously. I've waited all my life for that special woman and now that I've found her, blow me if I'm going to let her experience a moment's pain alone. You're hurting, and we aren't moving from this sofa until you tell me everything that is on your mind."

"Aubergine and split pea stew?"

"Jessamy?"

He used my full name. This is heavy-duty TLC.

I waved an imaginary white flag and curled up close by his side, resting my head on his waiting lap. "Okay. You win. It's been quite a day."

***

As expected, Lawrence took my account of the day's events in his stride. Throughout, he punctuated my sobs with perfectly timed strokes of my hair and attentive nurturing ums and ahs.

A hand wiped a stray tear from my cheek. "So why do you think it was all a dream? Sounds pretty real to me."

"Maybe I don't want it to be real? It's got to be a trick. I mean, I get that sometimes weird stuff happens, but here I am lying on the couch of the late departed Mr Moorfield and nothing. Not a peep of a flashback or a feeling. Nada. Zilch."

I bolted up, knocking Lawrence's elbow with my head, making us both say 'ouch!'.

"You have sharp joints, Mr Pixley."

"And you have a hard head, Reverend Ward. But don't change the subject. Have you actually tried to connect with the objects here? Don't you have to consciously ask for a sign or something?"

I grabbed the cottage embossed cushion and squeezed its corners tight and my eyes shut. Nothing. I threw the useless object at my fiancé's head. It bounced off onto the floor.

Lawrence bowed to pick it up. "Try again and this time with a tad more respect."

Chagrined, I took the cushion back and tried again.

"Calling the ghost of Greg Moorfield. Come in, Mr Moorfield!"

"Jess! Take it seriously. You've done this before. Why are you being so childish?"

Harsh words from a school master. There was no sticking a thumb in this dyke, the waters were rising and I couldn't stop them any longer.

"Because," I sobbed. "I don't want this. Any of it. I want you and my job and a quiet goddess free life. Is that too much to ask?"

"To be blunt, yes, it is." My flannelled knee felt the gentle comfort of his touch. His honesty, though, ripped right through my borrowed jogging bottoms and pulled at my insides. "They, whoever *they* are, have given you an extra-ordinary opportunity to help others, and that's what you really want, right? To help others find answers. To find peace. So this goddess psychic protector thing isn't what you expected when you came back. I get it. You didn't expect to find me here, either."

I went to protest his logic, but his raised finger made me pause.

"You're meant to be here on Wesberrey. All your life has been heading to this point. God has handed this cup to you. There's no saying no."

"Are you suggesting I am refusing God's will?"

"If my Sunday School serves me right. I think I am actually directing you to Matthew 26:39. And he went a little farther, and fell on his face, and prayed, saying, 'O my Father, if it be possible, let this cup pass from me: nevertheless not as I will, but as thou wilt.'"

Chapter and verse.

"Impressive." I sneered

Lawrence sat back, and with a knavish smugness that was extremely attractive, folded his arms.

"My love, we are going to be married. I'll be by your side, no matter what. Quoting the Bible, Star Wars, or scenes from The Breakfast Club if it helps you. The beauty of a wasted intellect is that I have a brain full of useless sayings I can pull down for any such occasions."

A relieved snicker escaped my lips, with a harmonising toot from my nose. *So, ladylike.* He was right. I was being a spoiled brat. Having offered my life to the service of others, I had a duty to use whatever talents I possessed to do so.

I placed the cushion on my lap and laid my hands, palms down, on the image of the cottage. After a few deep breaths and the now-familiar bout of nausea, I was standing in the centre of the room talking into a mobile phone.

"Lawrence, it worked. I am in the room speaking to someone. I don't recognise the voice on the end of the line, but it's male. English. Local. It's familiar but I can't place it. I am putting the note inside the cushion cover."

"Great. What are they talking about?"

"Oh, why is this so hazy? I think the treasure hunt? Greg's saying that he doesn't want to cause trouble. The other man is asking to meet. Seems this is all some big misunderstanding."

"What is?"

"Sssh, I don't know. The mystery man is suggesting popping down the beach hut for a chat, whilst it's still light. Greg agrees."

Lawrence squeezed my forearm. "The mystery man must be the killer. He knew Greg was going to the beach hut that afternoon. No one else did."

The sofa caught me as I collapsed back. "If only I could recognise the voice."

"Maybe you will. I think it's time to go back next door and tell the others what you know."

"And how I know it? Like to everyone?" I asked, knowing what his answer would be.

Lawrence nodded. "Honesty is the best policy. Right?"

I exhaled in reluctant agreement

"Yup, you're right, that's what they say."

Guess Who?

Rosie handed me a bowl of stew. "Jess, you are an idiot sometimes."

"Excuse me, but I can't be the only one here who thinks all this psychic nonsense is, well, nonsense."

The rest of the party looked at me and each other before collectively shrugging and moving on with the conversation.

"What? You all just accept this stuff?"

"Jess," Rosie raised her glass of merlot and used it to emphasise her words. "Look at the room. You are the only religious person here. The rest of us are open to suggestions. We grew up on Sabrina the Teenage Witch, Buffy the Vampire Slayer, and Doctor Who. We are the Star Wars generation and beyond. The Force be with you and all that."

Luke thrust a spoonful of split peas into his mouth. "Have you seen what trends on YouTube? Paranormal videos, ghost stories, and folklore. Vikings, Native Americans, and stuff. How many shows on Netflix are about magic? It's so cool that the women in my family have special powers. Who needs fiction when it's real? Right?"

"And if what you say Briganti said is true, then we all have the power within us." Tilly ripped apart a crusty bread roll and dipped it into her bowl. "Now, that is awesome."

Lawrence grinned from across the table. "Jess, see. We're all right behind you. As a headteacher with a talent for wrangling melodicas on a Sunday morning, I've listened to many sermons. Your predecessor spun a good line in inspirational thought. But, at the end of the day, though rooted in tales of the good Samaritan or the sermon on the mount, the message was always the same. Live in truth and love. Be kind to each other. Have faith. That goes for every belief system, ever."

They outnumbered me, these casual believers. These open-minded seekers of truth.

What am I so afraid of?

"But, what about Cindy?" I protested.

Rosie reached over her wine-free hand and tapped my fingertips. "And what about Ernest? Or anyone else reaching the end of their lives. Isn't it wonderful to know for certain that this is not the end? Cindy has known this since she was a child and still has wrestled every drop of joy out of her time here. She's had a glorious life. And now it's your turn."

I knew better than to continue to press the point. No one could understand the conflict that raged inside me. I wasn't sure I understood why it continued, despite all the evidence and all the experiences I had had.

Discovering the church when I was at my lowest ebb had saved me. I had found comfort, security and a purpose within its embrace. It was my truth. My home. My passion. Now it was only part of the answer. If I accepted what Briganti said, then how could I continue in my work and not want to share with everyone what I now knew to be real? How can I continue with a mantra of having faith when I had knowledge of the certainty of a life hereafter? How could I practise my ecclesiastical duties knowing they were unnecessary in the grand scheme? All we needed was love. Ritual was a distraction.

I need to change the subject.

"Right, so let's get down to business. I need to wrap this up ASAP. I have a wedding to plan. Now, how do we trap our murderer?"

***

Despite having organised a cosy incident room back at the vicarage, there was little point in hoofing it to my house, with everyone gathered here. Luke spread his photographs across the freshly cleared dining table, like the final stages in a game of *Guess Who*. Is the suspect male? Elderly? Grey hair? Tilly found some coloured index cards to record any clues. She marked up one card with Byron's name and another with a giant question mark.

She put them both on the table and checked our reactions. "Well, a proper investigation would look to eliminate suspects. We can't rule out the possibility that your uncle did it based on the evidence so far. And, who knows, there might even be a suspect we haven't considered."

The group gave a collective sigh of agreement. It was possible that Byron was the killer, no matter how ridiculous we all believed it to be.

Buck leaned across the table and picked up the card with the question mark. "Let's start here then. Is there anything at all that leads us to someone who was not a member of the Beach Squad?"

There followed a minute's silence.

"Well, then, this is dead in the water." He grabbed a red marker pen from his daughter's pencil case and drew a thick X across the card.

"We had to consider it." Tilly pouted.

Buck put a comforting arm around her. "I know, my dear. It was right to raise the possibility. And, as you said, we can now safely eliminate it."

Rosie was up next. "So, Uncle Byron. How do we know it isn't him?"

There followed an awkward shuffling of feet and allegiances.

"Because Greg Moorfield's ghost said so. Or rather, he didn't say, but it was clear it wasn't. And all the other Beach Squad members are certain it wasn't him."

Lawrence rubbed my shoulder. "But Jess, none of that will stand up in a court of law. Your psychic insights are great for pointing us in the right direction, but we need proof. Hard as it is to admit, at the moment Byron looks the most likely killer."

I tapped his hand in agreement. "I know. The murder weapon was a nail gun, and they found a nail gun at the scene with Byron's name on the base."

Rosie picked up Byron's card and tapped it against her lips, her mind desperate to find an answer to that riddle.

"Why would a grown man, who lives alone with his elderly wife, write his name on all his tools? It seems very childish."

"Well, of course at school parents do it so we can repatriate their children with their belongings. Maybe he was always losing things?" Lawrence chirped.

"Or things had a habit of wandering off!" I clapped. "Ken Wilson told me that everyone knew that Byron never locked his tool-shed, and many people would borrow his stuff simply by jumping over the hedge at the back of the garden. A footpath runs alongside."

Buck was unconvinced. "Wouldn't you buy a good lock and be done with it?"

Luke put his hand up, keen to jump in. I nodded at my nephew, who was bursting with insight.

"Byron didn't care about people taking stuff. He was happy to help anyone in need. Byron told me he trusted people would bring things back. He wrote his name on the tools to remind people where they got them from."

"Well, I'll be... your uncle is as crazy as a bullbat. He's made himself the perfect patsy."

Whilst Buck's words were full of Texan flavour, there was no denying that my uncle had created the ideal landscape for someone with malicious intent to set him up.

Rosie was growing defensive on our uncle's behalf. I could see her upper lip curling. A signal I learnt when she was a child meant she was pushing down some slight or injury. "I suppose the members of the Squad, his so-called friends, would know about his generous heart, but was it really common knowledge? I mean, I didn't know."

"Sis, let's be honest. We know little about any of our family, especially Byron. How many times have we sat down and spoken with him since we arrived?"

"But I know enough to know he's not a killer." She ripped up the card in her hand.

Lawrence took her cue to move on to the other suspects.

"Kenneth Wilson. From what you were telling us earlier, he was quite forthcoming. He was straight up about the treasure hunt. Which none of the others mentioned at all. And he told you about Byron's shed. Doesn't seem very sensible to provide your uncle with a 'Get out of jail free card' like that."

207

"And he saved my life. With a pikestaff."

Luke pulled out a chair. All this cerebral exercise was tiring him out. "But he was our number one suspect before, because of his background."

"True, he was a nightclub bouncer and a boxer. He's still very strong. Don't let his wiry frame fool you. I think if he had murderous intent, he would be more physical. This was planned. Like the phone call. Someone lured Moorfield out of his house."

"See, this is where I come unstuck." Tilly pulled out the chair next to my nephew. "Jess, if we are to believe that what you saw earlier is what happened, and we have no reason to doubt you, then why did Mr Moorfield agree to meet them before the treasure hunt?"

"Yeah," bounced off Luke, "why not invite them to come to his house half an hour earlier or something to clear the air?"

"You know what's funny?" Lawrence rested both hands on the table. "The murderer wanted the ambergris, right? And they shot the only person who knew where it was within feet of where it lay buried."

"So," I ventured, "they didn't give Greg Moorfield a chance to tell them where it was. Surely he would have pointed it out when faced with a nail gun to the forehead."

"Unless the ambergris is a red herring?" Rosie dangled a refreshed wineglass between her fingers. "I mean, we only knew about it because of Byron and good old Alfie here."

The faithful retriever, currently curled beneath Buck's feet, wagged his tail on hearing his name. Buck bent down to stroke his new best friend's ears before answering.

"And no one has been in Greg's house except us, from what I can see. Not even the police, which is strange."

"I guess they were waiting until all the fuss died down. The murderer, that is. Not the police. No point drawing attention to their motives when they have so skilfully steered DS Stewart in the wrong direction."

Lawrence shifted the photographs round. "All three of the suspects told a different tale about the ambergris. Wilson confirmed Moorfield's intention to give it away in a treasure hunt, but Cummings stated it was finder's keepers and Meacham that they were going to share the spoils."

Buck could smell a conspiracy. "Yah see, why do they have such different stories? To deflect and confuse most likely. Son, these photos. You took them outside the hut, and they were all together?"

Luke ran his fingers through his curls, pulling out the tangles in his memory. "Yes, sir. Like I said, I couldn't hear what they were saying, but they seemed in good spirits. Well, they weren't arguing or anything like that."

"I know we eliminated the question mark," Tilly pushed the crossed-out card back into the centre, "but maybe they had nothing to do with it. None of them seems on edge at all."

"Or they feel victorious!" Buck slammed his hand on the table. "Jess, are you sure you didn't recognise the voice on the phone?"

I dropped my head in my hands. Buck pressed harder, throwing suspect names at me over and over. His frustration was clear to see. It had been a long, thankless day for us all.

"We're just going around in circles." Tiredness was taking a stranglehold on my ability to think any longer. "I say, we sleep on it and if anyone can think of the perfect trap, we can discuss it tomorrow. I need my bed. Buck, are you okay with keeping the ambergris here overnight?"

"Yes ma'am."

And with that, we all wished each other goodnight. It looked like both Rosie and Luke were staying the night. *And it's not my place to judge.* Lawrence insisted on escorting me to my front door.

"Goodnight, my love." He stroked my cheek and leaned in.

I need to invest in some platform heels. My tippy-toe balancing skills are a tad unreliable this late at night.

Cat's Eyes

H ugo was mewing on the coir mat on the other side of the threshold.

"I'm sorry. Poor thing, you're wasting away."

As well as platform heels, I need to get an automatic cat food dispenser.

After filling his respective bowls with water and canned meats, I grabbed a few tins and a torch to take a late meal up to the churchyard, making sure the kitchen door was closed firmly behind me. Hugo is not a nocturnal creature, and wouldn't roam far, but I wanted to make this a quick delivery and get to my bed with no further drama. Chasing a black cat around the vicarage grounds in the moonlight was the last thing I needed.

A mesmerising dance of reflective amber and green lights caught in the beam of my torch. Purring their pleasure that it was finally dinnertime, their snaking ballet guided me up to the oak tree. I held the tiny flashlight under my chin as I opened the tins. Soft furry faces nudged my icy fingers whilst I spooned the food onto the trays.

I yawned several times. Yawns that sucked in the night air like a vacuum cleaner.

I can't wait to get to bed.

Most of the brown compacted gloop disappeared before I had finished emptying the can. I stroked the head of a ginger tom next to me. He was a burly chap with a scar across his eye. A greedy fellow with all the hallmarks of a leader.

"Now, you will let everyone have their share, eh?" I cooed before standing up to return home

That's funny. I could swear I left the lights on?

The vicarage sat silhouetted against the purple sky. I scanned the beam of my torch across the path and along the wall, looking around for signs of a power outage on the island as I walked. In the distance, I could make out the glow of the hospital.

How strange. I hope it's not a blown fuse. That's all I need.

Inside, I locked the kitchen door behind me. The switch was on the far wall and the fuse box in a cupboard under the stairs in the hall. I didn't want to stumble over a sleepy cat in the dark.

"Hugo?"

There was a faint cry.

"Hugo? Stop messing. Where are you?"

Another muted miaow and gentle scratching.

"Are you outside?"

I turned and opened the back door. Hugo, regal on the step, tilted his head and licked his lips.

"How did you wind up there? I was sure you were inside." I crossed back and hit the switch. The ceiling light came on straight away. "Strange, I must've turned it off when I left. Sorry, Puss, you had to dine in the dark. But then you can see in the dark, that's kind of a cat thing. Come on then, you sausage, let's go upstairs."

***

Usually, when there's a puzzle, my mind switches into overdrive the moment my head hits the pillow. But not this time. Tonight, the weight of my burdens and the stress of the day pulled me down into the mattress for safekeeping. I know I changed into my nightdress and set my phone to charge. I vaguely recall turning out the bedside lamp. But there was no room for thoughts of goddesses or ambergris, nail guns or flights through space and time. Just sleep. Blissful. Merciful. Sleep.

***

Seeing in the dark may be a useful feline talent, but pouncing on my chest before sunrise is an unwelcome species trait.

"Ouch! Hugo! Those claws! I'm up, okay?"

He leapt onto the bedside rug and paced back and forth in front of the door, hissing.

"What's got into your bonnet this morning? Your midnight stroll last night gave you a wanderlust, eh?"

I fell towards the door handle and opened a small crack to let him out.

"Fear not, Sir Fluff-a-lot, I will be along to serve you breakfast anon."

I crawled back to my bed.

Maybe I caught a chill yesterday?

I curled under the covers and hugged myself tightly. Shivers pulsed through my weary body.

Just a few more minutes...

"Vicar! Reverend Ward?... Oh my word, she's dead! Jess, can you hear me?"

I stretched and rubbed the drool from my mouth. "Barbara, of course, I can hear you. What's all the fuss about?"

Bleary-eyed, I reached for my phone to check the time.

My parish secretary planted herself at the foot of my bed.

"Oh, thank goodness." she panted. "When I saw the mess downstairs, I feared the worst."

I had a late night. Don't judge me.

"Barbara, sorry. I'll clean up in a bit." I pulled the covers around me. "Actually, I don't feel so good. Think I might have caught a cold."

"Well, you stay put whilst I call the police."

I grabbed the edge of her floral skirt as she stood.

"The police?"

"Don't you worry yourself," She placed the back of her hand on my clammy forehead. "You look like death. I will call PC Taylor and make you a cup of tea."

What are you babbling about?

I collapsed back into my linen cushion sanctuary.

***

Familiar voices called through the fog.

"I am sorry to hear the reverend is unwell, but you must appreciate that I have to talk to her, given the situation."

"Can't you come back later? I took her in a tea an hour ago and she hasn't taken a single sip."

"If she's not up for questioning, then I suggest you call in the doctor. I can't leave here without a statement. And we will need to dust for prints, etc. DS Stewart will be along shortly."

Detective Sergeant Stewart?

"Who's out there?" I cast a look at the lukewarm tea on the table beside me.

"Just me, Reverend Ward, with PC Taylor. He wants to ask you a few questions"

"About what?"

I struggled out of my cocoon and pulled on a dressing gown hanging over the dressing table chair.

PC Taylor's head greeted me in the hallway as I opened the door. He sought an explanation from Barbara. "Hasn't she been downstairs yet?"

I pushed them both aside. "No, I have not. Can't a girl have a morning's peace in this place?" I turned down the stairs towards the morning room. "Barbara, I'm sorry. Can I trouble you for another cup of tea? Constable Taylor, would you like a drink? Let's take this downstairs."

My head throbbed as I held the banister. My feet appeared to have lost all their bones.

I want to go back to bed... the sofa in the morning room will have to do.

"Oh, my G—!"

A shiver ran down my spine that had nothing to do with my cold. A scene of utter devastation spread out before me. Sofa cushions lay tossed across the room. The base of the couch gaped open. Someone had taken a sharp object to my soft furnishings. Cupboard drawers hung open-mouthed. Their contents were strewn along the floor.

I grabbed onto the door frame for support. The room spun. Fortunately, Barbara was there to catch me. I took refuge on the stairs, folding myself into the wall to stop from falling in a heap at the bottom.

"All the rooms on the ground floor are the same." PC Taylor flipped open his notebook. "Didn't you hear anything?"

I glared at him from under my heavy lids. "No, I didn't, Constable."

Barbara fussed. "Well, I take that as a blessing. Lord knows what these hooligans would have done to you if you'd disturbed them."

The lights? Hugo? The back door?

"Where's my cat?"

Barbara squeezed beside me on the stairs. It was a tight fit. "He's okay, I let him outside for a bit."

"Constable, last night... I think they snuck in whilst I was feeding the colony and waited until I had fallen asleep."

"Do you have any idea who 'they' are?"

"No. But I think I know what they were looking for. Whale vomit."

Perchance to Dream

"So you see, DS Stewart. It can't be my uncle. The killer is still out there and is looking for the ambergris."

Toddler-like, I rocked on the bottom stair. I feared my legs wouldn't be able to get me back to my room, so I had paused there to rest, and it was from this lowly position I had given my statement.

DS Stewart's tailored trouser waistband towered over me. *Such a flat stomach! Impressive for a woman of her age. She must work out...*

"Reverend Ward. Am I going to have to arrest you for obstruction?"

"No!"

Jess, stay focused.

"I swear, we were going to tell the police everything today. You know, I nearly drowned yesterday!"

"So you said. You were contemplating life after visiting one of your flock. Who just happened to be your uncle's friend, Kenneth Wilson. And, I might add, a person of interest."

"Yes, he saved me."

"Of course he did. With a civil war pikestaff. PC Taylor got all that down in his notebook. One thing I don't understand, Miss Marple, is what you were doing poking around in an active crime scene. Didn't you see the blue and white tape?"

"Around the beach hut? Yes, but it was Alfie who led us to the ambergris. On the beach. Outside. Not inside."

Fingers crossed the Boss would allow one tiny white lie, in the circumstances. If he is still my boss?

"I see. Let's say I believe you didn't break a police cordon." She folded her arms, her legs astride. "Your first thought after finding buried treasure was to break into the dead man's house and look for a key. You could have turned the box in then. Before you went on your little swim?"

"Yes. Well, Alfie was thirsty.

"This is Mr Moorfield's dog."

"Uh-huh. Just as well Buck took him in. Your lot hasn't been anywhere near the house. The poor creature could have starved to death."

"Oh no, Madame Poirot. This is not how it works. I investigate the crimes. You spout myths from the pulpit. I don't tell you how to write a sermon, now do I?

I shook my head. Bad move. It took a while for my dislocated brain to settle afterwards.

"Surely, the break-in proves my uncle is innocent."

"It proves he either had an accomplice, or someone else is interested. That's all." She turned to PC Taylor and tutted. "I think you need to pay Messieurs Wilson, Cummings, and Meacham another visit. So, Sherlock Holmes, you say the whale vomit is at this Buck's house?"

"Yes. He'll hand it over. I swear." I raised my hand in a mock pledge. "You should pop into Moorfield's bungalow whilst you're there. He has a son. In Australia."

"We are very well aware of that fact, Reverend Ward. I suggest you get back to bed. You really don't look at all well."

***

The moment DS Stewart left, I asked Barbara to fetch my mobile phone and called Buck so that he knew to expect the Spanish Inquisition to land on his doorstep within the next few minutes.

Bang went our bargaining chip. Without the ambergris, it would be impossible to lay a trap. Not that I was in a mood to play Scooby-Doo. Hot and cold waves rippled through my body like they were playing a weird game of ping pong.

The second I pressed the end call button, Barbara bundled me back upstairs.

"I'll be clearing up downstairs if you need anything. Old Reverend Weeks had a bell. I think it's in the study somewhere. I'll bring it up. No more vicar-ing or sleuthing for you today, missy. Bed and some hot broth are what you need."

"Really, Barbara, I'm fine. No need to fuss."

Barbara hung for a few seconds in the doorway. "I'll call your mother as well. I bet she makes a grand chicken soup.

Great, that's all I need.

I plumped the pillows into a triangular pile behind my back. I may be off duty, but I could still use the time to walk through the clues again. My mental faculties, though, refused to play ball. On several occasions, I startled myself back awake.

That voice. I know that voice. I know it well. If only I could recognise that voice on the phone...

**

"Jess, my darling, I came as soon as I could."

I creaked open one eye to spy Lawrence leaning over me with a cold compress.

My mouth was desert-dry. "Water, please," I croaked.

A cool glass met my parched lips. I took a sip.

"What time is it?"

"Just before four. I had meetings I couldn't get out of. How do you feel?"

"Like a human crash dummy. Everything aches."

"Then you need more sleep. I'll tell your mother you are up, though. She's keen to get some food inside you. Sam was here earlier. She's prescribed complete bed rest."

"Sam was here? I don't remember."

I must've been really out of it.

"And Barbara? Is she okay? She had quite the shock earlier. Is anything taken?

Lawrence shook his head.

"Broken?"

He bit his lower lip and examined the scroll pattern on the rug on the floor.

"They knocked over a glass fish."

"Don't tell me, the orange and teal one on the sideboard?

No! That was my favourite!

***

Lawrence retreated to his home to collect some overnight things, handing over fevered brow mopping duties to Mum, who had come up with a tray of warm goodies.

"Thanks. What did Sam say?"

"To rest and stay hydrated." Mum fussed over my bedding and pushed a couple more pillows behind my back for support.

"But what about Uncle Byron? I have to solve this."

Mum turned to the window and drew the curtains. "*We* have to solve it. I've spoken to Rosie, and she updated me on what you were up to last night." She flipped on

228

the bedside lamp. "I've also had a few choice words for Pam. She should never have taken you to meet the goddess. You're not ready. Mentally or physically."

So this is some sort of post-space travel virus. Like the bends?

"She wanted me to know the truth, I guess."

"That's as may be. She's not thinking straight right now. When you feel better, and Zuzu returns, we will work on this together. Strength in numbers. You're not on your own. Anyway, I heard they're releasing Byron on bail. So, we have time."

"That's great news." My head bobbed forward. My eyelids fought hard against my desire to stay awake.

"Come on, eat up, then you can get back to sleep." Mum rested another pillow on my lap and placed the thin wooden tray that held my bowl of broth at the centre.

"Okay. It smells wonderful. Is that sage?"

"Nothing brings out the flavour of chicken better. Also good for cleansing bad ju-ju."

I paused. My pursed lips hovered over the spoon. "Is there any magic in here?"

"The only magic ingredient I added was love. Now, hurry before it gets cold."

***

A fresh storm rattled my bedroom window. The original Georgian frames were a key feature of the vicarage's charm, but they were draughty, especially when the weather took a turn for the worse.

Mum came in to collect my tray. "Not very pleasant out there. Good thing Barbara called off the PCC meeting tonight. Let everyone stay snug in their own homes."

"She didn't need to cancel it!"

"Well, until you appoint two new churchwardens, there's very little point in Barbara and Phil leaving the pub on a blustery evening to sit with old Rosemary in a freezing church hall, now is there?"

"Not without me there, I guess not. But it's premature to ask for volunteers to replace Tom and Ernest." I straightened myself up. I must have been sweating at some point, my pyjamas clung to me and I smelt like a musty old sea dog.

Mum positioned herself on the edge of the bed. "Is it? I would have thought you would need someone in post as soon as possible, what with Christmas around the corner." She brushed some imaginary fluff off of her trousers. "And, you being busy with the wedding and all?"

Oh, no! Rosie has a big mouth.

"I was going to tell you. Or rather, Lawrence and I wanted to tell you. Both together. Then, well, it kind of came out the other night. We were so excited. Lawrence got a little carried away. I'm sorry, Mum."

"It's okay, really. I understand."

It isn't, and she doesn't.

"I suppose you expect me to wear a hat. I'll look like the Queen."

"You wore a hat for Rosie's wedding. It was very fetching."

"Yes, and look how that turned out."

"Mum, I said I'm sorry. You can help me pick a dress."

"Hmm. It's a good thing I like Lawrence. His mother, though. All preppy hockey sticks. And tall. I can't compete with that." She marched to the curtains and tugged them, though they were already closed. I knew she was trying not to cry.

"Mum, I really am sorry. You have always been the most beautiful woman in the world to me and I don't see that being any different this Boxing Day, do you?"

She sniffed a tear onto the back of her hand. "I see you are still delirious. I'll get you some more broth."

***

Flustered voices climbed up the stairs from the hall. Slow, deliberate footsteps followed. Their owner's heavy breath grew more laboured as they approached my door. I scanned my bedside table for a weapon. A glass of iced water? It will have to do.

The door inched open.

"Oh Rosemary! You frightened the life out of me." I placed the jug back down carefully.

"Sorry, Vicar. But your mother told me to come straight up. Wanted to check in on you, that's all. I didn't get the message about the meeting. My silly old ansaphone. A carrier pigeon would be more reliable."

"I'm afraid I'm not much company, but I don't think I'm contagious. Just a slight fever. Caught a chill, you know."

"Well, attempting to swim on the far side of the island will do that to you." Rosemary hovered at the foot of the bed. Her hunched shoulders barely held her neck up.

I patted my bed covers. "Make yourself comfortable. Those stairs are steep."

"I'd rather stand if you don't mind, Reverend Ward. If I perch on that mattress you might need a crane to lift me back up." she laughed. "Now, I hear you've been talking to my cousin."

"Well, I spoke to all three members of the Beach Squad."

Rosemary grimaced as she shifted her body and shuffled her feet from side to side. I patted the bed sheets again, but she insisted on standing. "Oh, I know, Reverend. Roger popped over this morning for a chat. Said Ken had to pluck you out of the sea. He wondered if I'd heard how you were. He seemed extremely concerned about your welfare. You must have made quite the impression upon him."

"That's nice to hear. So, you see him often then?"

"Not usually, no. In fact, I can't remember when I was last so popular. He came over Saturday night too.

"On Halloween?"

How intriguing...

My interest was most certainly piqued. It was time to get out of those sweaty sheets. I swung my legs out to the side and searched the floor for my slippers. The draft from the window was a welcome surprise on my bare shins, its bracing touch a relief from the claustrophobic weight of the feather duvet.

"Rosemary, I think you need to sit down in a sturdy chair whilst we have a nice cup of tea. Here, take my arm. You can hold me up on the way down."

Bonne Nuit

Lawrence arrived back just in time to insist on phoning for a horse-drawn taxi to take Rosemary back home.

"You can't be too careful with a murderer on the loose, Mrs Reynolds."

My rickety organist tapped my fiancé on the chest. "No need to worry about me, Mr Pixley. You take care of the vicar. I see you're staying over." She planted a purposeful nod at his overnight bag. "Very wise. After everything that has happened."

I wheedled in under Lawrence's arm and squeezed him tight. "And Mum is going to be here as well to keep me topped up with broth. Aren't you Mum?"

"Of course, my dear." My mother paused. A mischievous smile wrestled with the corner of her upper lip. "Rosemary, has Jess had time to invite you to play the organ on her big day?"

"No, my dear, but of course, I'd be delighted. How sweet of you to ask me. I'd say June's the perfect time to tie the knot on Wesberrey. There's still plenty of blossom on the trees and everything else is verdant green."

Mother's revenge has begun.

"I still have to ask the Archbishop," I coughed, "but we're actually planning on holding the ceremony on the 26th of December."

Rosemary's head recoiled on her bowed neck like a python. "This year? How avant-garde. Maybe it will be the whitest of white weddings. The snow I mean." A blush rose in her pearlescent cheeks. "Come along, young man. As this was your idea, you can walk me down the path. The taxi will be here soon."

As the front door closed behind them, Mum dragged me into the morning room.

"What are you thinking of getting out of bed and sitting for an hour in that kitchen with barely a stitch on? Don't you want to get better?"

"I had to find out what she had talked about with Roger. And she could hardly breathe after you made her climb all those stairs. What were you thinking of?"

She paced in front of the fireplace. "I was hoping you would stay in bed as you were told."

"Mum, please sit down. You're making the place look untidy." I joked.

"Haha, you got that line from me." She caved, dropping on the high-back chair opposite me. "What did you find out?"

"Roger Cummings surprised her with a visit on Saturday evening. She hasn't spoken to him in months. They only ever talk when they bump into each other in the market or somewhere. He never visits. Anyway, it seems he also popped in again this morning after he heard I went to talk to Kenneth Wilson. Wanted to know how I was."

"That's very suspect." Mum rubbed her chin. "Why the sudden interest? Perhaps he thinks his old cousin isn't long for this world and wants to make sure she remembers him in her will."

"Or he needed an alibi. He made a point when I was at his house of making sure I knew Rosemary was his cousin and that I should talk to her about his moral character. When I mentioned that to her in the kitchen just now, she was most surprised. She said she really didn't know much about him. They are cousins. But she'd moved away when she got married and when she returned after her husband died, Roger had joined the army. She didn't see him at all for over twenty years, except at odd family gatherings, and even then he didn't socialise much. She always thought he looked down his nose at everyone."

"Bizarre to give her as a character reference, unless he knew he needed someone."

"And she also confirmed that as far as she knew he never progressed past sergeant, He certainly wasn't an officer."

Mum relaxed back into her chair and gestured *'well, that's it'* with her hands. "So he's a liar and shifty with it. Byron should be back home tomorrow. Maybe he can help a bit more in his own defence."

She rose wearily and dragged her slippered feet towards the hall.

"I'll head off to bed now. Give you alone time with lover boy. But Jessie, please get some rest. You still look peaky," she waved her hand around my face. "Especially around the eyes."

***

Lawrence returned from his stint as a boy scout to become a much-appreciated masseur.

"I hope you're not expecting this level of treatment when we're married." he quipped. "Once that gold band is on your finger, I expect you to provide me with my pipe and cocoa by the fire every evening."

"I noticed you left out home-cooked meals."

"Jess, every good fantasy has to have at least one foot in reality."

I slapped his hand. We both giggled.

"Beloved, I would kiss you very hard right now, but you have the lurgy. I draw the line at sharing germs."

"But you always have a handkerchief on standby."

"For my allergies. Nothing else I can do to fend them off. But I don't need the plague, thank you very much."

I went for another playful slap, but my hand decided it would be more beneficial to curl its fingers under his and grip tightly. "Maybe it's not a virus or a chill. Maybe I am having a massive reaction to the cats. I fed them late last night."

Lawrence rested his chin on the crown of my aching head. "Nonsense. You've grown immune. It's fascinating really when you think about it. Your body has adapted to Hugo, whereas mine still goes crazy with the merest hint of tree pollen, or dust, or horsehair or..."

"Horse? But not cats?"

"No, but then we used to have cats, and the island is full of them. I imagine you weren't allergic when you were a little girl?"

"You're right, I don't think I was... hold on but, your garden has trees. You can't be allergic by your own logic. It's all in your head."

Lawrence released my neck and took up the chair Mum had sat on earlier.

"Fir trees," he smiled. "We have only evergreens. Nothing with any blossom. No flowers, no pollen. Dogs are fine, too."

Fascinating as this discussion was, I needed to change the subject. My brain was working at fifty percent capacity – certainly not enough to fill it with an analysis of potential allergens.

"Byron's got bail."

"I heard. So, my *petite fleur*, who do you think did it?"

"Ooh, I love it when you speak French. I wish we were back in Paris." I wriggled into a crossed legged position on the sofa, hoping the more active stance would help my brain function better. It only served to knock my voice into a pompous accent.

"Well, M'lord, let's consider the evidence... I believe all three of the Beach Squad are in it together and are deliberately weaving differing stories to confuse us."

"Hmm, I get it looks that way, they are acting suspiciously." Lawrence paused. "And Luke saw them talking together by the beach hut yesterday. But then, they had lost a friend, even if he was little more than an acquaintance. Surely Moorfield's grisly demise struck them hard. And with their long-time friend accused of murder... I think, in those circumstances, I would meet up as well."

"I guess if one of them acted alone, keeping up the pretence of caring as much as the others do would help cast suspicion elsewhere." A nagging thought pecked behind my right temple. *The voice on the phone.* "Maybe we should head to bed soon. I feel like I have a small bird trying to escape from my skull."

"Of course, let me help you upstairs."

My legs buckled, and I dangled like a sack of potatoes in my fiancé's arms.

"Not the most ladylike of swoons." I giggled.

Lawrence scooped me up and, doing his best not to bump my extremities against doorposts and the banister rails carried me to my room.

"Does M'Lady need anything else before I retire?" he bowed.

"Is a goodnight kiss out of the question?"

He took my hand and pressed his lips against my knuckles. "*Bonne nuit, mon amour.*"

The Morning After

I would like to say that sleep brought with it murder-solving visions. That, dancing in between the ghoulish characters of my slumber, helpful nocturnal pixies offered me slavers of juicy clues to chew on over breakfast.

I would love to say that.

Instead, I remembered nothing after my head fell against the freshly changed pillowcase. Mum had been busy before she went to bed. Clean linen cocooned me - cool, crisp and smelling of lavender. All things considered, I spent a quiet night embracing empty thoughts and healing vibes.

The morning, however, found me slumped over the kitchen table, wrapped in a crocheted shawl, a bowl of steaming porridge warming my hands. A good night's sleep had failed to cure me of this freakish malady.

Lawrence was heading to work. "I'm going to ask the British Legion to help with assembly tomorrow morning. They usually have volunteers selling poppies there, anyway. The school drop off is a good time to catch the parents and the kids love it."

Of course, it's Remembrance Sunday this weekend. I had work to do. Actual day job stuff, not goddess whispering and amateur sleuthing.

"I can still lead the assembly as planned, but having someone from the Legion talk would be wonderful."

Lawrence smirked as he cast a knowing glance at my mother. *They're in cahoots!*

"Well, it's always wise to have a backup plan, dear." Mum handed my beau a brown paper bag. "I'm sure these aren't as good as the ones your mother makes."

What have I just witnessed?

"Lawrence! Does your mother make you a packed lunch every day?"

My fiancé thanked my mother and turned to go. "Not every day." He winked and blew me a kiss.

He winked!

As the door firmly closed behind her latest project, Mum turned her attention to me. "I'm not sure you're ready for married life."

"Not if it means waking up at the crack of stupid to make sandwiches. No, you're right." Taking solace in the steam spiralling from the bowl before me, I did not lose the irony of my petulance. I was a pampered princess with no right to judge what I had just seen.

A stray droplet of water found an escape route along a lower lash. More followed like lemmings jumping off into the oat sea below.

"Jess, sweetheart, I don't think you're ready for any of this. Perhaps you should take everything a little more slowly?"

A salty pool formed on the skin of my milky breakfast. "I want things to be normal. So much has changed. And still is changing. It's never-ending. The ground beneath me is quicksand. Every few weeks there's something new. A fresh revelation, a surprising gift, another dead body!"

The legs of the chair screeched as Mum pulled closer. "And you've been amazing. I can see now that I was wrong to remove you from all this. This is your destiny. Instead of learning, as I did, as my sisters did, that this is our way over a lifetime. You're now on fast-forward. Hurtling to the inevitable at record speed."

"You did what you thought was best. I understand that. You were grieving and wanted to protect us. I'm just being a big wuss about everything. And that is not our way. Our way. The way you taught me, is to pull up my big girl panties and soldier on. And that is what I need to do."

Mum put an uncharacteristic arm around my shoulders, squeezed, and pulled away in one fluid motion. "I suggest you have a shower first."

***

Barbara had cancelled all my duties for the day, which gave me plenty of time to pull myself together for a visit to Aunt Pamela's house that evening. As the day drew on, my symptoms thankfully subsided to the level of a middling cold. The sweats stopped, and the headaches subsided.

By mid-afternoon, I found sanctuary in my office looking for wedding dresses on the internet. I hoped that the distraction would help my recovering mind work out what to do next. We had no bait for a trap and zero evidence to point us in any direction above some general misdirection and hunches.

Luke had popped in over lunch to add the photos and index cards to the corkboard in the spare bedroom. Both he and Tilly were working in the pub that evening, and it seems Buck had an urgent business meeting on the mainland. Rosie, of course, was busy at D & V.

Everyone was getting on with running their lives.

Mum went home to change her clothes and, as she said, do her own chores, leaving me to ponder the case alone. To be honest, it was a welcome relief.

I left the lure of cream lace behind, grabbed a fresh cup of caffeinated nectar, and positioned myself cross-legged on the bed facing our incident board. Luke had done a wonderful job. Coloured wool threads linked clues together. Index cards summarised what we knew and raised further questions. Polaroid photographs of the suspects held centre stage. All three men appeared to have the opportunity to murder Greg Moorfield, but nothing was standing out as a motive. Apart from the ambergris.

To my right, I noticed that a fold in the bedspread was inching towards me. As it drew closer, the fabric mound arched and circled. There was the slimmest of possibilities that it was something spookily paranormal, but my guess was it was most likely an unamused black cat.

The cloth-covered hill stopped and purred under my right hip. I patted Hugo's blanketed body with my cup-free hand. "So, Puss-puss, do you have any suggestions? Could you talk to Alfie for me? Maybe he knows who did it?"

Hugo barely stirred.

"Of course, how silly of me. You would never lower yourself to talk to a dog." The devoted golden retriever's cheery face stared back from the corkboard. *Why didn't Greg take Alfie with him?*

Hugo's paws edged out from below the bedspread and then, with ninja swiftness, clawed at my thigh, causing just enough of a scratch to make me recoil towards the headboard.

"Ouch! I was being nice, you little devil. Watch yourself, or I'll trade you in for a Yorkshire Terrier."

Dogs are so loyal. *Didn't everyone say Alfie was Greg's constant companion?*

I grabbed my phone, kissed Hugo on the head, and dialled.

"Rosie? Do you have a few seconds? I just want to run something by you. What if Greg took Alfie with him and the murderer brought him back to the house to help find the ambergris?"

I could barely hear my sister over the barista machine.

"Sure, Jessie, I'll bite. But even if he did, how exactly does that help Uncle Byron?"

Good point.

"I don't know. But the cliff walk would have been filled with dog walkers at that time, right? Late afternoon before it got too dark. Perhaps someone would remember Alfie if we walked him along that same path again at the same time? Dog walkers are creatures of habit."

"That'll be five-pound-fifty, please. Thank you."

"Rosie, are you listening to me?" I snapped.

"Yes, of course, I am, but I do have a business to run."

The bang, bang, bang of a metal coffee frother ripped through my fragile head.

"Sorry, I just want to get to the bottom of this."

"Jess, it sounds like a great idea. Now, you go back to bed, or I'll tell Mum on you."

A threat I suspected my baby sister would take much glee in carrying out.

"Where is Alfie now?"

"Home alone, I guess. Buck is on the mainland."

"Yeah, right... Okay, we'll talk more tomorrow. Love you."

Man's Best Friend

Poor Alfie, cooped up indoors all day. The fresh air would do both of us the world of good. I could return Buck's running gear as well. Mum had washed them along with my sweaty sheets and nightwear. All I needed to do was work out how I would get into Buck's house.

Or maybe I don't have to? Has Tilly left for work yet?

There was only one way to find out. I called her.

"Hi, Tilly, glad I caught you... Yes, I'm feeling much better, thanks. Erm, are you still at home?"

I had wandered back to my room and was trying to insert my left foot into my trouser leg using crafty footwork and my free hand.

"I just thought Alfie will be needing a second walk what with your father on the mainland and all. And I could do with the exercise... Yes? Great, I'll come straight over. See you in a few minutes."

I was not sure what I had planned other than to walk Alfie back up before sunset and see who we bumped into. Walking the dog also gave me the perfect alibi for poking around on the beach again. I was missing something and maybe spending more time with Alfie would help me connect more strongly with Greg. He must have taken the dog with him. It was still light when he took the call, and Alfie was due for his evening walk soon after. Kill two birds with one stone, so to speak.

So, I would get the spare set of house keys from Tilly. Walk Alfie for a bit and then, maybe, casually slip back inside the Moorfield residence and see if I can find anything else. Anything at all.

Did Greg have his house keys on him? What happened to his personal effects?

My educated guess, that I shared with Hugo as I continued to get dressed, was that the killer met Greg on the beach, murdered him, took Alfie and the keys back to the house, then slipped around the estate to join the fellow members of the Beach Squad outside the front of the house minutes later, thereby creating for himself the perfect alibi.

A simple 'home' command had set Alfie bounding back up the house. Maybe the soppy animal didn't even realise his master was dead. He only began to howl as the house grew dark and he realised he had been left alone. *Maybe dogs aren't as loyal as we think...*

The look on Hugo's face as I locked up suggested that he thought that dogs were quite stupid.

***

"Oh, I wish I could come with you." Tilly waved in the direction of Alfie's leash with one hand whilst, with perfectly framed eyes fixed on the hall mirror, she applied a careful smear of cherry red to her cupid's bow using the magic wand she held in the other.

She caught my fixation on her ability to multitask in the mirror's reflection.

"Too much?" she asked.

"Not at all. You look stunning. I was never very good with make-up. Even stage make-up, back in the day. I always looked like Coco the clown."

"I'm sure it wasn't as bad as that. And the top? It's new. What do you think?"

I think it is designed to show off your ample wares. Does it really need to be quite so low cut? Jess - listen to yourself!

"Also stunning. The colour really brings out your eyes."

"Not too tarty, right? Do you think Luke will like it?"

"I think Luke will love it!"

"Great." Tilly moved to the bottom of the stairs and pulled across a pair of black platform Mary-Jane shoes. "Did you know that we are both thinking of applying to university? He was saying we should talk to Freya about moving further away. But I want to stay here, to be honest. I have only just found my father and this is my first proper home. Stourchester Uni is commutable, and we both have good jobs here. And family. I don't see the point of uprooting again. What do you think?"

"I think you should consider all the options. You don't have to go to the same place."

"Oh, but we do. I can't imagine being without him." Shoes strapped on, Tilly stood up and smoothed down her top, admiring herself for a final time in the mirror. "You're right, it really does bring out my eyes. Anyway, the keys are on the hook. The ones for here and next door. Just put them under the terracotta pot by the bin shed when you leave."

She grabbed a jacket from the banister pole and added. "I do love our little family. It's all just perfect, isn't it? Right. I better get off or Phil will have my hide. Happy sleuthing."

***

The walk down to the beach was uneventful if you don't count the dozen or so times I got Alfie's lead caught around my ankles, or the near-death experience I had when he decided to leap off a ledge a few feet from the bottom. *Hugo is right, dogs are stupid.*

Fortunately for my dignity, the beach was almost empty. Not so great for finding witnesses to the crime who might recall an elderly man and his dog out on an early evening stroll on All Hallow's Eve.

As no one was around, I let Alfie off his lead and strolled as nonchalantly as possible around the crime scene. The coastal wind had dragged most of the police tape up onto the rock face behind the hut.

Why had none of my visions shown me Greg's assailant?

The tide was going out and Alfie was doing his best to catch up with it. I would call and he would come walloping back, each time a little more covered in mud. I found a smooth stick, perfect for throwing, for him to chase. He was easy to please.

I sat on the veranda of the beach hut and stared out at the cargo ships on the distant horizon. In the past, such vessels would sail closer inland looking to unload their cargo on Stone Quay. Now the harbour saw little trade, with yachts heading straight to the marina and fishing boats finding their moorings on safer shores. The absence of cars secured the demise of merchant shipping on Wesberrey. Why moor across on the other side of the island and unload onto horse and carts when a few nautical miles up the coast on either side you could access docks with direct access to the country's motorways.

A shiver ran down my spine like an icy pole had been drawn along my back. The sun was making her bed ready for the night. It was time to retrieve the retriever and head back up the path. Night falls quickly at this time of year. Greg must have been here around four, any later and it would have been too dark. Even with a torch, this would be treacherous.

I called Alfie, who bounded back and then within a few feet of my waiting hand, dashed at a ninety-degree angle away down the beach in the opposite direction.

Stupid dog!

I ran after him and followed his tail around a hidden bend in the sea wall.

Ah, this is what you're after.

A cute wooden shack, smaller even than the beach huts, with a candy-cane awning pulled out over an open serving hatch, stood snuggled beneath a chalky overhang. The owner was shutting up shop, but the pictures pinned up on its shutters announced he sold ice creams, sweets and *candy floss.*

"Hello boy, haven't seen you in a while"

Alfie weaved his golden body in and out of the proprietor's legs. They were clearly well acquainted.

I called across. "I see you and he are old friends."

Alfie's best buddy uncoiled himself and stretched out a hand to greet me.

"Pleased to meet you, Larry Collins, purveyor of the finest confectionery on the whole of Wesberrey. I don't believe we have met, though, I must say your face looks strangely familiar."

"I'm the vicar from St. Bridget's. Maybe you've been to church?"

"Nah, that wouldn't be it." He removed his straw boater and scratched his bald head. "This thing gets mighty itchy, but it all adds to the brand. Image is very important in this business. The punters expect a certain level of bonhomie."

"I guess they do. I wish I had known you were here earlier. I see you have some toffee apples. Very festive. I used to love them as a kid."

"Tell you what, if you promise to tell your congregation to pop along here after mass this Sunday, I'll give you one, even two, for free. Can't say fairer than that now, can I? Just give me a second to open up."

"Sounds like a deal, Mr Collins. Though I'm not sure I have time to hang around right now. I still have to walk back up the cliffs and the light is fading fast."

"You are new here, aren't you." he laughed. I'll give you and Alfie here a lift back to the vicarage if you want. My wheels are parked just up the slope there. There's more than one way onto the beach."

Of course, there is! How stupid can I be?

"Mr Collins, I am sure you heard about what happened to Alfie's owner on Halloween."

"I did more than just hear about it. I heard it."

"You heard it!"

Larry must be the witness.

"Well, I heard a conversation. The wind here carries words off to the sea as soon as they're uttered. Normally I can't hear anything that happens further up the beach. It's a struggle sometimes to hear what my customers want. I have learnt to read lips if I'm honest. But, I told the police there were several voices. All male."

Larry unlocked the side door and reached inside for a toffee apple. "Here you go. Now if you just give me a few minutes to fire up Mr Whippy I will give this gorgeous fella his favourite treat, bless him. He must be traumatised by it all."

"Thank you. Did you see who was talking?"

"No, only Alfie here. He ran over as I was packing up. Then Greg must have called him to go home 'cos he dashed off."

The ice cream machine juggered into life. The refrigeration unit was noisier than I expected.

"So, you didn't hear it was Mr Moorfield then?" I shouted over the machine.

"No. I told the same to the police. I couldn't make out who was there, but given what happened next Greg must have been one of the voices, right? And I suppose the others were his friends, you know the Beach Squad."

"But you're not sure it was them, or how many of them?"

Larry nudged me aside to grab a cone wafer. "No, but who else would it be? With the storm brewing, very few people were on the beach that afternoon. It's why I have so many toffee apples left. Trade wasn't as brisk as I'd hoped."

The whipped cream spiralled down onto the cone through the metal nozzle. Alfie's tongue stole most of the treat before it landed.

"Easy, fella," Larry gently pushed the eager hound back towards me, and I grabbed his collar and reattached the lead. Order restored, the ice cream rose to a satisfying point, and Larry crouched down with Alfie's reward. "There you go, champ"

The grateful hound woofed it down in one.

"So, there was no way, Mr Collins, that you would have identified my uncle as the murderer."

"You're Byron's niece! That's why your face is familiar. He used to share whenever you were in the Stourchestershire Times. He is very proud of you, Reverend Ward."

Is he?

Larry washed his hands and dried them on a nearby cotton dishcloth. "I'm pretty sure it wasn't Byron. To be honest with you, I don't see how any of those old men could have done it. I mean, they're a bit strange. Aren't we all? But murder? Nah."

"But if not one of them, who and why?"

Larry ushered me and Alfie back out onto the beach.

"I haven't the foggiest, and if I had I would tell the police straight away. I liked old man Moorfield. He always popped by the shack and bought something for himself and Alfie here. I'll miss him. One thing though, that has been bugging me..." Larry distractedly turned off the ice cream machine. "As I said, I couldn't make out much of what they were saying. It was menacing, though... And I could swear one of them had an accent."

"An accent? What? French? Italian? Northern?"

"Not foreign, foreign. You know what I mean. I didn't catch much, but ... maybe it was just the wind. It plays tricks, you know."

That Man

I rode up front in Larry's ape van with a sticky Alfie wedged in between us. Within minutes there was dog drool all over the dashboard. We stopped outside the vicarage. I stepped down, carefully holding tight to Alfie's collar as I dragged him out behind me. "Thank you for the lift. Sorry about the mess."

"Pleasure to finally meet you, Reverend. Byron has told me so much about you. I know you are a bit of a detective on the side, so to speak, so I hope you get to the bottom of this. I really do. I wish I could be more helpful."

"Who knows Mr Collins, your insights might be just the thing to break this case wide open."

"That's the spirit, eh. And don't forget to tell your parishioners I'll give them all a two for one on toffee apples on Sunday. A Remembrance Day special, if you like."

And with a tip of the brim of his boater, Larry Collins chugged away into the dark.

I turned to drop off the toffee apples in the kitchen to see Mum standing, arms folded, in the doorway.

She tapped her foot. "And where do you think you've been?"

"Just getting some fresh air. I got you a toffee apple. See?"

Mum was unimpressed.

"Well, go get yourself ready. I guess we can drop the dog off on the way."

What way? Oh, yes, Uncle Byron was being released on bail.

"Of course. Sorry. Won't be long. Do you think I have time for a bath?" The stern folds on her forehead told me she was losing her patience, and fast. "A shower it is then."

I ran up the stairs to find a fresh set of clothes laid out on the bed. Mum had obviously been back some considerable time – hence her mood. She always busies herself when she's anxious.

In the bathroom, I ran the shower and took a breather on the toilet. I had to think through what I had learnt, and it was the only place to sit. *Multitasking at its finest.*

If Larry Collins is the police's only witness then their case against my uncle is circumstantial. A decent lawyer would be able to argue that it was common knowledge that Byron was generous with his tools. In fact, it was a direct consequence of this giving nature that led him to write his name on them to begin with. They did not know about the ambergris until I told them, so what other motive did the police have? And if the ambergris was the reason for Moorfield's sudden demise, all four surviving members of the Beach Squad had the same motive, means, and opportunity. They were all gathered outside Moorfield's around six, but Moorfield was dead two hours before that. Any one of them could have done it.

How can I alert the police to the need to check Greg's phone records? That should lead them to the murderer. There was nothing else to go on.

Susannah had not gotten back to me yet. *Very frustrating.* She must have spoken to Dave by now.

As to Larry's assertion that one of the men had an accent, I was certain the voice on the other end of the phone was local. The more I thought about it, the more sure I was that he was not only a Wesberrey resident but a native. That would eliminate Paul Meacham and Ken Wilson, both Londoners. Roger Cummings was very keen to ensure he had a character reference in his cousin, Rosemary. He was lying about his military career. Maybe he had something else to hide?

***

On the way to Pam and Byron's house, my mobile phone rang. It was Zuzu.

Finally

"Hi, Jessie. Can't speak for long, but Dave found out who the witness is. A gentleman named—"

"Larry Collins?"

"Hey, how did you know? Don't answer that. Yeah, Dave said that his statement doesn't prove anything and, just between us, the Baron has some deep concerns about how the case is being handled. The problem is that it would be seen as a conflict of interest for him to get more involved. He did say he would have a private word with his superior when we get back. I understand Uncle Byron was released on bail, so..."

"Yes, we're on our way to visit him now. I am sure anything brought against him will be thrown out of court. If it even gets that far. Tell Dave, not to worry. Oh, except, if he can get his team to look into Mr Moorfield's phone records the night he died, that would be great."

"Is that Susannah?" Mum yelled into my ear. "Tell her, she can also call her mother sometimes."

Mum is in a foul mood this evening.

"Did you hear that?" I held the phone out and put it on the loudspeaker.

"Yes, I heard. Can Mummy hear me now?" Zuzu asked.

"Yup. She's all ears. How's the country estate? Everything good with you and the twins?"

"Dave's children are adorable. They love me, naturally. His mother is... how can I put this... a fascinating woman."

Mum leaned in and lifted the phone closer to her mouth. "I hope you're behaving yourself. We may not have had different forks for the fish course at dinner, but I brought you up to have good manners."

"Mum!" I snatched back the phone. "Sorry, Sis. I think we're all a little on edge. When are you back?"

"Sunday. Can't wait to be honest. It's very 'Above Stairs' here, talk about bor-ring." Putting on the baby-ist of voices, Zuzu added, "And Mummy, I have been on my best behaviour. Promise."

Mum tutted. I turned off the speaker and waved at my mother to go ahead without me.

"Sorry about that. It'll be great to have you back. I've missed you. Also I need your help picking out a dress. We've set a date. The twenty-sixth of December. This December."

There was an unnerving silence on the other end. *Surely I haven't scandalised Zuzu?*

"A Christmas bride! Oh, Jessie – you aren't hanging around. Excited to unwrap Lawrence's special presents, eh? I get it. Don't know how you have hung on this long, to be honest. That's one hunk of a man you've got there, little Sis."

She paused for a response. I declined to entertain her.

"Anyway, got to dash. I have to dress for dinner here. Can you believe it? Mwah, love you and congratulations."

After putting my phone back in my coat pocket, I pulled up my hood and walked as fast as I could to catch up with my mother. There was a frost in the air that night. The steam from my mouth could extinguish any dragon, except, perhaps, my Aunt Cindy who greeted me at the door.

"Darling! The rest are all inside, fussing over that fool Byron like he had just won the lottery. Can I grab a few words before we go in?"

How can I deny her, knowing what I know?

"Cindy, if you are mad at Aunt Pamela for taking me to meet the goddess, I'm sure she didn't mean any harm."

"Hush, child. Of course I'm not mad. She was right, I have been too, what's the word, enigmatic. Anyway, my darling, I merely wanted to check you had fully recovered. Beverley said you didn't handle the trip very well."

"I'm not sure it was that. I did get soaked to the skin, twice, as well that day. I probably caught a chill. Nothing more."

"Well, it doesn't change the fact that I've been remiss in my training. Your mother didn't want me to overwhelm you. It's a lot to take in and, to be honest, I thought you were doing a marvellous job on your own. Being a vicar and all that, you were more than halfway there already."

"No need to worry about me. It's you we have to take care of. I need you to stick around as long as possible to guide me. Look at you, still as nimble as a twenty-year-old. I say we work together to stave off this nonsense for as long as possible. You have a whole lot of life left in you yet."

"Oh, don't you fret, darling child. I'm not going anywhere, anytime soon. Too much to do here. Like making sure that silly old man is able to walk you down the aisle in a few months? He can't do that if he's checked into one of Her Majesty's special hotels."

Of course, who else will give me away?

Inspired by talk of good manners and Above Stairs, I offered my arm and bowed slightly. "Shall we?"

My radiant aunt gently placed her right hand on my elbow, and we glided into Pamela's floral print sanctuary.

***

Pam had been in the kitchen all night if the spread on the coffee table in the centre of the room was any indication.

Excessive catering aside, it was a welcome, if unusual, sight to see Byron hold court in his own front room. He appeared to be enjoying the attention. Perched on the armchair holding a plate of cake fancies and triangular sandwiches he spun his tale of prison life.

Pam hovered around like a hummingbird around nectar, swooping in and out every few seconds offering more tasty treats or asking if anyone needed some more tea. Her agitated state was so at odds with the calm, time-travelling goddess wrangler of the other day. The worry of the past week was etched deep across her face. She needed her husband to know how relieved she was to have him home. It had to be the perfect homecoming.

Mum was talking to Rosie on the sofa. Cindy went to join them, and I made my way over to pledge my fealty to this man of honour.

"It's so good to see you back home, uncle." I rested one bottom cheek on the left arm of the armchair.

"Only on bail, they said. Still think I'm good for it, Jessamy. Have you found out who did it?"

"No, sorry uncle. This one appears to be eluding me. I did find out though, that Larry Collins heard voices that night. He was pretty sure it wasn't you. Can I ask, where were you around four o'clock on Halloween?"

"Me? I was in my shed. Halloween is not a night to be around the sisters. I'm sure I told you this before."

"But you went to Moorfield's for the treasure hunt later on, right?"

Byron stuffed a meat paste vol-au-vent in his mouth. "Yes, but he wasn't in."

"But you didn't tell me that before. All four of you rock up outside the victim's house, and you didn't think it was important."

"Well, it was hardly an alibi as all four of us were there. Arrived within minutes of each other. That dog of his was already barking. I didn't know it then, but I just surmised the murder must have happened earlier."

The doorbell rang.

"That must be Buck." Rosie motioned to my aunt to let her answer.

Mum pulled my sister back. "Why would it be Buck? This is a family affair."

Rosie brushed her off.

"Rosie, I mean it. This is no place for that man."

That man? I never knew Mum had reservations about Rosie's new boyfriend. It wasn't like my mother to be reticent about how she felt about someone. But I recognised the term '*that* man' of old. My mother was harbouring serious reservations about my sister's relationship.

Rosie rushed to answer the door regardless.

Male voices carried down the hallway, not one of them had a Texan drawl. Rosie led them into the lounge.

"Uncle Byron, you have visitors."

It was the Beach Squad.

A Bad Feeling

"I say we leave the men to their cigars and adjourn to the other room." Cindy slipped a comforting arm around her oldest sister's waist and led the way into the kitchen.

Pam opened one of the wall cabinets and grabbed a tall tumbler. "I don't feel comfortable leaving him alone with them." She pressed the mouth of the glass against the door and her ear against its bottom.

"Does that trick actually work?" I whispered,

"Well, I'll be able to find out if you all stopped talking." Pam placed a finger over her lips. "Can I get some quiet, please?"

We tried, but the silence didn't last for long. Rosie was the first to break ranks. "Mum, what did you mean earlier, about Buck?"

Confronted, Mum sunk back into an unconvincing state of temporary dementia. "I don't know what you are talking about. Hush now. Your aunt needs to concentrate."

"Oh no, you don't play that batty old lady nonsense with me. I caught your drift. You have a problem with Buck. Come on, spit it out."

Pam glared back at the bickering pair. "She doesn't trust him. None of us do."

"Well, that's news to me." I sidled over to my baby sister. "Buck has been a good friend and makes Rosie very happy."

My aunt sighed, removed the glass from her ear and looked at her sisters for support. "Time for a family conference. They're only talking about model railways anyway."

I sat close to Rosie at the far end of the kitchen table as the Charmed sisters lined themselves up on the other side.

Cindy took charge. "Rosie, my darling, how well do you really know him? I will give you he's very charming."

"And handsome." Pam piped in. "I can see the attraction. Especially on the rebound from Teddy, but he did abandon his daughter. Rather convenient coming back now she's a grown woman. Hardly the actions of a responsible parent."

"He didn't know her mother was struggling. He's trying to make amends now. We all make mistakes." Rosie's voice quivered.

"Darling," Cindy placed her hands on the table. Her sisters' hands soon joined her. They were united, as one. I could sense a change in the room's energy. Whatever this was, this intervention, it was not good. "Darling child, please take a breath and connect with us. We can only see the truth through your eyes."

Rosie recoiled. Her hands backpedalled into her chest. "I'm not doing this. Buck's a good man. Jess, tell them how he has been helping you. I don't need a witchy Google search to know he genuinely cares about me and Luke. He adores Tilly. He regrets so much of his past."

Mum shook her head. "A past, which by his own admission, led him to crime. Has he told you what he was in prison for? More to the point, Rosina, has he told you what he does now?"

"Rosina? So I'm in big trouble then." Rosie's chair screeched as she stood up. "You know, Mother, if you were so concerned, why didn't you say anything sooner, eh? We have been going out for months! You just can't bear for anyone to be happy. To have a better relationship than you had. Just because your husband was a lying, cheating dirtbag, doesn't mean every man is."

Mum flinched but soldiered on. "Teddy was a lying, cheating dirtbag. I don't want you to be hurt again. I think it's all too soon. You have to grieve a lost marriage."

"What, like you did? Pulling us away from all this. Our family and friends. And acting as if none of it happened. That I didn't see my father choose death over staying with me!" My sister marched up and down in front of the sink, tapping the end of the counter with her fist.

I went to stand, but Mum flagged me to stay seated. I wanted to comfort Rosie. My baby sister who I played with on the stairs whilst my parents argued in the next room. The sister who slept in my bed whilst Zuzu snuck out at night to find a boy, any boy, to get back at my father. The little girl who cried as she made up stories for her dolls or screamed when I refused to leave the comfort of my books to help with her letter to Santa.

I loved her.

The pain in her heart ripped through mine like a teething puppy with a new toy. Yet, as I absorbed the energy in the room, I knew that the *Charmed* were onto something. Maybe Buck wasn't all that he seemed, but that didn't mean he would be out to hurt my sister.

I reached out my hand to Rosie, who took it and swung my extended arm back and forth like she did when I used to walk her to school. "Mum, Pam, Cindy, help us. What is it that you see?"

The sisters stretched out their fingers so that their tips touched. Cindy beamed. This was what she did best. The air pulsed around us. "Please join us. Is it not better to know than to have so many questions?

I stroked my sister's hand. "Rosie, only if you want to. My experience of all this so far is that it always leaves me with more questions."

My sister shuffled her feet and bit her lower lip. A china plate on the dresser to her side now seemed to hold all her attention. "That's a scene of the vicarage, right? Of the land and the cliff before they put up the railing."

"Yes, it is," Pam spoke softly. "A local artist. Victorian. Can't remember his name. It hasn't changed much really. That view."

"No," Rosie's voice was wispy. Her mind was elsewhere. I tightened my grip as if I had to hold firm to stop her drifting off into the night. "You're right, it hasn't changed. You are always right."

She looked back down at me and squeezed my hand.

"I think I knew."

Knew what?

"Rosie, sit please, You're not making any sense."

She did as instructed, though left the chair where she had pushed it back earlier, maintaining the distance our arms had bridged.

"When PC Taylor came to pick up the box. I know you had called ahead, but I thought it was strange. Buck didn't invite him in. They went outside and talked by the gate. I was upstairs. We had been, well, we've been dating for months now, you know."

"Okay, I get the picture. So you looked out the window?"

"Yes, I was curious. After all, that whale stuff was all we had to trap the murderer, and we were just handing it over to the police. Which, I know was the right thing to do, but... it was just Buck seemed relieved. Happy, almost."

"Well, given his background, I can see why he would be conflicted about holding back evidence from the police. It doesn't look good."

"I guess, but it was more than that. I can't explain it. They had quite a long conversation. Buck even slapped PC Taylor on the back a few times, which, I don't know, just seemed over-familiar."

"Nerves? We all do things out of character when put on the spot."

"Maybe, but there's something else. That night. The night you had the break-in."

"The night before, yes."

"Buck disappeared. Usually, after we, you know, he is out for the count for hours. But, well, it was all very rushed and I thought maybe it was the stew. Too many split peas, perhaps. Anyway, he got up to go to the toilet and was gone for ages. I must have fallen asleep because I didn't notice him getting back into the bed. Which he must have, right?"

A knife twisted in my stomach. "Sis, are you trying to tell me that you think Buck broke into the vicarage? That's crazy. He already had the ambergris. I mean, why?"

"To cast suspicion elsewhere." We all turned to see Byron standing in the doorway. He must have been listening to us the whole time.

***

"PC Taylor! The voice on the other end of the phone! I knew it was familiar!"

How could I be so stupid?

The half-baked police investigation, the slow pace of interviews, the lack of a police presence at Greg Moorfield's house.

The 'foreign' accent must have been Buck's!

Alfie readily ran home at his command. It all fits.

But we have zero evidence.

"Rosie, where is Buck now?"

"On his way back from London I imagine. Jess, it can't be true. I mean, he can be secretive and, under all that Texan bravado, he's often a little guarded. But... He can't be a murderer."

By now the whole of the Beach Squad had gathered in the kitchen.

"I really hope not, lil Sis. It's unthinkable. Poor Tilly. And Luke. We must be wrong. It's our overactive imaginations feeding off the excitement of Uncle Byron's release."

Byron had lost no time updating his friends on our suspicions. "Much as I would love to put someone else's name in the ring for this, there is something we're still missing. A motive. What on earth could your Buck and PC Taylor have been up to that was worth taking Greg Moorfield's life?"

Ken Wilson had the answer. "Smuggling."

"Smuggling what?" I wondered.

"Drugs, cigarettes, alcohol, people."

"I'm sorry," blustered Roger Cummings, "but I can't see that clod Taylor being the head of some human trafficking ring."

"Well, it's always the quiet ones," Paul smirked. "He's probably been at it for decades. He was the only copper on the island for years. He could have gotten away with murder, well maybe he has."

The room fell silent.

Paul Meacham bent forward and scanned the strange gathering. "My money's on people. One of the fishing boats picks them up at sea and brings them to shore where they are met by what's-his-face and Officer Plod, and they take them in a waiting vehicle up the slope to a safe house. There they clean them up, dress them as tourists and then simply walk them off the island on the ferry. In the height of the tourist season, no one, not even eagle-eyed Bob McGuire, would notice a few more passengers departing than had arrived earlier. It's really quite beautiful. Why would you be suspicious of people leaving the island? No customs, no border control. It's a risk, but a very lucrative one, I would imagine."

"How do we accuse an officer of the law of smuggling and murder without any evidence?" Rosie looked around the kitchen. "Because we don't have any, remember? I saw my boyfriend chatting with him as he handed over a metal box. That proves absolutely nothing."

"You're right, Sis, and yet all the pieces fit together. I don't want to believe it, but something is telling me this is the solution. Uncle Byron, have you ever lent Buck your tools? Perhaps when Rosie was decorating D & V?"

Byron closed his eyes and shook his head. "No, but PC Taylor has had loads off me in the past. In fact, I don't think he's ever brought one back. The little snake."

"Chaps, I say we come up with a strategy of attack. Moorfield must have seen something on the beach. Most likely, as Meacham says, in the current global economic climate, the illegal transportation of people, but it could have been barrels or boxes of illicit contraband."

"I think you have something there, Roger. Maybe Moorfield saw this Buck fellow you keep talking about. His neighbour, right? And your lover. So sorry, miss. You seem like a lovely lass. This must be hard."

"Thank you, Mr Wilson." Rosie had dragged her chair back to the table and was now determined to solve this mystery. Her anger and pain had solidified into a stoic resilience. She appeared to me, in that moment, the personification of that famous British stiff upper lip. Somehow, if I cut her in two, like a stick of seaside rock candy, she would have the words 'Keep calm and carry on' in rings around her centre.

Remembering how she had built up her business and put up with Teddy all those years, I imagined she had learnt to fake a smile and do whatever needed to be done. She was the least deserving of this scenario, and yet here we were, facing the very real possibility that Buck was involved in the murder of his neighbour.

Paul Meacham suggested a rota to camp out on the beach and look out for any suspicious activity. "Hopefully, we will catch them in the act."

"And then what?" Ken retorted. "They will have accomplices. I imagine at least a couple of handy geezers to handle the merchandise. How do you suppose a bunch of old men and women, no offence ladies, take them on?"

Pam got up and strolled over to the kitchen sink. "I think I should put the kettle on. Good thing there's plenty of food. We're going to be here for a while."

A Cunning Plan

And we were there for a long while. Whilst we schemed, Buck called Rosie to see where she was. He had a surprise for her. My sister, arguably a better actress than I ever was, told him she had a headache from an unusually busy day in the cafe and she would call him in the morning.

So far, so good.

Roger Cummings relished the opportunity to lead our battle plan and soon three rotas were drawn up. One to watch the beach, one to keep an eye on PC Taylor and the other to stick like glue to Buck.

"I'll take the lion's share of that," offered Rosie. "I'll call one of you whenever he's not with me, so you can pick him up."

We all agreed.

"And what do we tell Tilly and Luke?" I asked.

Pamela, restored by a cup of Ceylon blend and a plan to save her husband, was clear. "Don't tell them anything. Act as normal. We need to lure the culprits out. Too many of us know as it is. Tilly is going to be hurt in this, no matter what. No point in causing that pain any sooner."

***

My mother and sister came back with me to the vicarage. Neither of us wanted to leave Rosie alone with her thoughts. There was still a strong possibility we were wrong and somehow we were being gaslighted by the actual murderer, a member of the Beach Squad, into wasting our time following other suspects. Yet, something in our cores told us we were right.

How could PC Taylor have remained hidden in plain sight for so long? Though, as Meacham said, he was the only police officer on Wesberrey. He didn't even have a police station. If all other crimes remained low key, then there was no reason for the Stourchestershire Constabulary to get more involved with the day-to-day to-ing and fro-ing from this little island.

"Do you think that's why Buck bought a house here?" Rosie had curled her legs up on the sofa, using a cushion for comfort. "To support PC Taylor? You know with all the murders and stuff drawing unwanted attention. Inspector Lovington moves in and then you turn out to be this great crime-fighting vicar. They had to find a way to get closer to you and Dave. And they did that through me." Rosie wiped the remains of her tears off on the back of her hand.

"And he used his own daughter, the man is scum." Mum kissed my sister on the head. "I think you should try to get some sleep, dear."

"I'm not sleepy, Mum. You know, so many things make sense now. His private phone conversations. His office being out of bounds. Did you know that? We should go there and break-in. There will be plenty of evidence. Jess, didn't you put the key under the pot? We could go now—"

"Buck's back home, remember? Let's keep an open mind. Maybe all or none of that is true. As Pam said, we carry on as normal and see if they slip up. Dave will be back on Sunday, and we can hand over whatever we have discovered to him then."

"Hmm," Rosie dug her nails into the cushion, "provided I don't kill him first. People, Jess. It's people. What he is dealing in. People. I know it is. I just know."

***

The next couple of days passed peacefully. I taught the Remembrance Day assembly, feeling like the worst fiancée in the history of time for not telling Lawrence what was going on. The group had made a pact. Others had to maintain even harder poker faces.

Rosie received, with feigned delight, the gold pendant Buck had bought for her whilst in the big city. She allowed for a kiss or two but found excuses for anything more intimate, promising something extra special on her day off on Sunday.

Tilly and Luke were actively encouraged to work extra shifts at the Cat and Fiddle. And when anyone asked about the Beach Squad, we told them that without the ambergris, there was nothing we could do and to leave it to the police.

As to the police, believing her man to be on bail and with no reason to look at any other suspects, DS Stewart had moved on to other cases. PC Taylor was left in charge. The world, on the surface at least, appeared to be back to normal.

Except, there was a huge fireworks display planned to take place on Saturday night in the grounds of Bridewell Manor to celebrate Guy Fawkes night. A curious English custom of lighting a huge fire and sticking the effigy of a traitor on the burning flames. The event at Bridewell was one of the largest in the country and saw a sharp increase of day trippers to Wesberrey from the mainland. An extra late ferry was laid on to take people home afterwards.

The group surmised that if people were being kept somewhere on the island awaiting their turn to leave, Saturday night would be the perfect opportunity to move them on.

Roger Cummings took sentry duty from a vantage point he had scoped out earlier in the day. With military-grade infra-red binoculars and a set of walkie-talkies, he maintained communications with his fellow Squad members. Paul had elected to mark PC Taylor. He had been trailing him day and night and had his suspicions about the location of a possible safe house. The problem with a solo twenty-four surveillance mission is there is little time to go back and check such suspicions out. Ken was keeping his eyes on Buck.

Rosie had decided to keep D&V open until fifteen minutes before the fireworks were to begin. Mum worked with her, whilst Pam and Cindy went up to the manor house to watch the display. Lawrence and I were to join them there.

Byron was staked out at the beach hut. We had all bases covered.

Buck had popped by the cafe earlier in the afternoon. When asked if he was planning to go to the event, he said that he wasn't a great fan of large explosions. Too many drunken Fourth of July celebrations. And, he needed to stay at home for Alfie. Dogs are frightened of fireworks.

Strange how this conversation would have washed over my sister if it had happened a few days earlier. Now, she was messaging everyone in our shared WhatsApp group convinced he was going to move his merchandise that night.

I hope we are right, if wrong we have destroyed their blossoming relationship and my sister's heart for no reason.

***

Bridewell Manor stood wrapped in a clear orangey-violet sky. The perfect backdrop for crackling bonfires and wheezing rockets of gunpowder.

The grounds were swarming with bobble hats and scarves of an autumnal hue. Anyone wanting something meatier to eat than the fare on offer at Dungeons and Vegans could find more than enough to tempt them at one of the pop-up stands dotted along the path to the central attraction – a large stack of dried timber, old scaffolding planks, and unwanted wooden furniture ready to be set ablaze.

Across the lawn, local lads poured plastic cups of cheap beer over the grass and themselves as they pushed and jostled for the attention of the gathered young ladies by the marquee. All to the soundtrack of nineties drum and bass from the Manor's PA system. The central reserve was home to families with small children, many holding multi-coloured light sticks.

When I was young, we were trusted with sparklers. A white-hot metal wire packed with magnesium and other such explosive materials at one end. *I'm sure these coloured lights are safer, but they can't be as much fun.*

Lawrence and I found my aunts taking prime position on a raised podium by the fire. The smell of grilled beef and charcoal merged with old wood and dust invaded my body through every pore. Soon, everything would smell burnt, not just the burgers.

My pocket vibrated. I reached in for my phone.

Ping. A WhatsApp message, from Rosie.

R: Ken's lost him.

J: Who? Buck?

R: Yes. He just called in at the shop. Buck walked Alfie on the park area on the estate with the other walkers. Ken hung back, watched him go back to the house and he's gone.

J: Where eis he now?

R: Dont know. Hes gone.

J: I menat Ben. Ken. aagh. Autocorrect !

Darn, this thumb typing in the dark is hard work.

R: Gone to join Roger.

J: Roger that.

R: What? Roger what?

J: No, I menat, blast. I'll call you.

I made my excuses and walked away from the hubbub to call my sister back.

"Hi, Rosie? That's better. How does Ken know he's not in the house?"

"Because he could hear Alfie whining. Can you see PC Taylor? Is he at the fireworks?"

I cast my smoke-filled eyes around, but the light was not ideal for spotting a navy policeman's helmet in a sea of wool. "He was here a second ago... Darn it."

Lawrence pulled up beside me.

"Jess, what's up? You are acting really strange."

"Rosie, hold on." I covered the mouthpiece and looked up at my handsome fiancé. "Let me take this, and I'll tell you everything, I promise."

A muffled announcement grumbled over the tannoy. They were about to light the fire.

"Rosie don't do anything stupid. I'll be right there."

"Right where? Jess, what in heaven's name is happening?"

I took Lawrence's hand and explained everything to him as I dragged him back out through the crowd.

Some bright spark quipped "You're going the wrong way, Vicar. The witch burning's that way!"

No time to respond.

In the distance, fireworks began to whizz and bang. Squealing like frightened mice as they spiralled upwards into the night sky creating cascading rainbows of light. The noise around us and the height difference between us meant that Lawrence didn't properly hear what I was trying to say until we were several yards outside Bridewell and running along Upper Road.

"So, Buck is the question mark."

"The what?" I shouted back.

"The question mark. On the index card. No wonder he was so keen to eliminate the mystery suspect. Couldn't risk us asking too many questions. Colouring outside the lines, so to speak."

"Lawrence, I love you desperately, but this isn't a time for riddles. I need to get to my sister before she does something stupid."

I thought about going back to the vicarage to grab Cilla, but it was downhill all the way, and I didn't have time to fiddle with helmets. The adrenaline rushing through me was positively powering me down the street like Usain Bolt. Even Lawrence with his long legs was struggling to keep up with me.

We rounded into Market Square to see Mum standing distraught outside the cafe. "I tried to stop her. I've never seen her like this."

Lawrence wrapped a strong arm around her.

"She's angry. Mum. She's not thinking clearly. Did she head to the ferry?" I asked.

Mum nodded into my fiancé's chest.

"Darling, stay here and look after my mother. No wait, take her to the Cat and Fiddle. When I find Rosie, I'll bring her back there. We need to keep Tilly out of the way too. This could still be one great, big mistake."

I *knew* it wasn't. I knew Rosie had the same feeling too. I can't explain the connection, but her soul was telling her the truth, and her heart sought revenge. Even without a scrap of evidence, we *knew* Buck was involved and this wasn't going to end happily ever after.

But no time for deep philosophical reflections on the nature of intuition. This sixth sense was driving my sister towards someone who, more than likely (if this sixth sense is to be trusted) is happy to buy and sell innocent people.

I got to the ferry port. It was pitch dark save for a light in the captain's cabin.

Ping.

R: Vicar what are you doing? Get away from the ferry.

I looked around. Roger was positioned well out of sight. I should have taken a walkie-talkie. The internet is patchy on the waterfront.

K: Come to the train station. Rosie's here.

Thank you, Lord!

I used the phone's torch to make sure I wasn't stepping off the harbour wall into the sea. Last time I tried to apprehend a murderer on Harbour Parade, I had ended up having an unexpected swim.

"Jess!"

I turned. "Rosie? What were you thinking? Mum is worried sick."

"I know, but the more eyes on the ferry, the better I figured. I mean Buck or PC Taylor might not be the only ones involved. We need to be looking out for anyone who appears frightened or nervous. You know." She pulled me into the station office. Tom was on duty. He looked tired.

"Tom? Couldn't anyone else do this tonight? It's so late."

"Oh, I volunteered. One of the youngsters wanted to go to the display. All his mates were going. You're only young once, eh, Reverend. And as much as I love the bones of that man, he is driving me mad." Tom attempted a weak smile. "Anyway, the hordes will be descending soon enough. Have been having a lovely chat about pugilism with Ken, here. He's also brought me up to speed on the situation. You know my lips are sealed. PC Taylor, eh? Who would have thought he had it in him? Heh, Ernest is missing all the fun."

I edged away to catch up with Ken. Though in my heart I knew Buck was our man, there was still the chance this was all a setup. The Beach Squad could be having a great laugh at our expense.

With Mr Wilson there was no time for pleasantries. "So, how did you lose him?"

"I promise I only took my eyes off him for a second, But, well I guess I am getting a bit too old for this malarkey, eh? But we'll get him. Roger's got eyes on the ferry. We'll move out when the crowd comes. And Meacham called in about twenty minutes ago. He's still got PC Plod in range. Says he went into an old chalet along the back of Upper Road. Just as Paul suspected. Not been rented out for years. Only has half its roof following the big storm of '87. Rather suspicious behaviour if he's not trafficking, don't you think?"

I had to agree.

The bell rang for the train car to ascend. Ken rubbed his hands together. "This is it. Keep 'em peeled."

Rosie, Ken, and I fanned out away from the station. Roger radioed in that the swarm was on the move. *I guess Operation Beehive or The Sting or whatever we call it in our memoirs has begun.*

The packed train car descended. Bobble hats and scarves chattered as the first party snaked their way to the ferry. There was nothing suspect about the next two cars either. But by the third descent, the crowd started to swell with groups who had managed to get a cart down and then the walkers.

It grew harder to keep an eye on the crowd and my sister. *This is insane!*

Then I heard her voice. I don't know how, over the rhubarb, rhubarb of the gathering throng, but it was Rosie, but... where was she?

"Here, over here. It's Buck. I can see him, the bastard."

I stepped on my tip-toes to find her. I only found a sea of heads.

"It was you, wasn't it. Where is he then? Your accomplice."

Rosie?

Panic rose and strangled my words. I couldn't see her. *The voice, her voice, must be some telepathic radio wave.*

People kept passing by. One dark winter jacket after another. Parents carried small children on their shoulders. Lovers walked like conjoined twins, not looking where they were going, just following the flow. Drunken young men held each other up, waving scarves, and cheering loudly.

Where is my sister?

There was a hard bump, and some radio cackle. "Cummings has eyes on her. They're on the ferry." Ken barged through the revellers. I piggy-backed on his coattails, literally. There were too many people. Too many.

We funnelled into the waiting ticket line.

"There, look! I almost didn't recognise him without his helmet." Ken pointed in the direction of the Square. It took me a few seconds to see what he could but standing behind a group of about five or six young women was PC Taylor.

Behind him – Paul Meacham.

Psst-click. "Meacham has eyes on the copper. Over."

"Got him. Over."

"Looks like he is heading to the Texan. Still have eyeballs? Over."

"Roger, that. Over. Come on, Vicar, let's get to your sister." Ken elbowed travellers out of the way, left and right. "Emergency. Make room. Clergywoman coming through."

As we neared the edge of the dock, we could see Bob McGuire corralling passengers to check their tickets. Ken pushed me through to the front of the line.

"Bob? Have you seen Rosie?"

"Yes, she's on the bow with that Yank," he growled.

"Okay, erm, Bob. Can you see PC Taylor over there? He's out of uniform, but he's under the lamp to the left. See?"

Bob nodded.

"Look, I don't have time to explain it now, but don't let him, or those women that he is with, on the ferry. Okay?"

"Vicar, if they've got a ticket." He shrugged.

"Bob. I need you to trust me. Ken, here, will help you restrain PC Taylor if you needed. Or can you just stop letting people on. For a few minutes? Please."

"Vicar, the tide is against us. It's late."

"Bob, I need to get to Rosie. She's in danger."

That got his attention.

"I'm coming with you. Here, Mr Wilson. You're in charge. Tell them I need to... check the pump."

He handed the rope over to Ken, and we made our way through to the front of the ferry. Rosie was arguing with Buck, far too close to the outside railing for my comfort. *What is she thinking?* With Bob bringing up the rear guard, I edged closer.

"Buck?" I shouted. "The game's up, please come quietly. The ferry isn't going anywhere. We have people watching PC Taylor. We don't know everything, but we know enough."

"You don't know jack, lil lady." Buck grabbed my sister around the neck and pulled her down, sliding her across the wooden bench as he backed his way to the railing. "I'll jump, and I'll take her with me."

I matched him step for step. Rosie wrestled to get away.

"Buck, you don't want to do that. What about Tilly? She needs her father."

"She doesn't need me rotting in a prison cell. The house is paid for. There's a trust with her name on it. She'll be fine."

"Fine. You're a great dad! If you want to die, go ahead, jump. But let go of my sister."

Buck threw his head back and let out a raucous laugh.

Rosie sunk her teeth into his wrist, and the laughter stopped.

"You lil bitc—"

Buck swung Rosie to the ground. Bob leapt from behind me and rugby-tackled her assailant to the floor. Once he had his prey pinned down, he pulled his right arm back behind his head and punched Buck so hard across his jaw, a tooth flew across the deck. He was out cold.

Rosie crawled up to her saviour and planted a huge kiss on his cheek. Bob collapsed back against the bench. A very happy hero.

A Day of Remembrance

The Last Post echoed across Market Square.

Wreaths to remember the fallen were laid beneath the First World War memorial at the front of the Guildhall by representatives of a grateful community.

Lawrence had stood by my side as I conducted the prayers for the Remembrance Sunday parade. Beside him, my mother and next to her, all in black and wearing her poppy upside down, a world-weary Tilly.

A humiliated DS Stewart had travelled over, with a small army of more senior officials, on the first ferry to take Buck and PC Taylor into police custody. The concussed Texan had awoken to find 'Captain' Cummings had comman-deered his corrupt accomplice's own handcuffs to secure them both in his basement until the authorities arrived. In contrast, their 'cargo' had spent a more comfortable night in a family room over the pub.

To her immense credit, Tilly had taken the terrified and confused young women, warm drinks and blankets and refused to leave until she knew that they were safe in the care of social services.

She is an incredible young woman.

The service over, we walked down to the harbour's edge, as it is the custom on Wesberrey to throw our poppies into the water in memory of all those lost at sea.

"Tilly? Lawrence and I were talking earlier, and... I know you have a lot to process right now, but we were thinking... Would you like to move into the vicarage? We can move some of your things in after lunch."

"Thank you, Reverend, but I couldn't possibly..."

I took her arm and brushed a curl away from her wet lashes. She had been crying and who would blame her.

"Yes, you could. Listen, if it makes you feel better, you can help me with the housework. Just warning you, though, I have very low standards. And, well you already know how bad my cooking is."

A sliver of a smile brushed over her lips. "But what about Alfie? I can't —"

I looked at Lawrence. "And he can come too. I think, in time, Hugo will learn to tolerate him."

"I won't stay forever. You will want the place to yourselves after you get married." She sniffed.

"Well, you'll be off to university soon enough."

"Yes," she sighed, "going away, seems the better option now, don't you think?"

***

Poppies solemnly sent on their way, I called across to Rosie, who had struck up quite the conversation with a certain fist-wielding ferryman.

"Hey, Sis. I know a great little place where there's a special on toffee apples. Fancy joining us?"

"No, I'll catch up with you during the week. Bob and I are going to grab a drink at the Cat and Fiddle."

Bob McGuire, I think she knows you're alive now.

What's Next for Reverend Jess?

ENSHRINED EVIL

It's Christmastime, but amongst the mince pies and tinsel, there are plenty of mysteries to keep Jess busy when she should be planning the most important day of her life!

In the final story in the series, Reverend Ward has to find a missing mystic and deal with the bitter rivalry of the local girl guide and boy scout troops, as well as arrange Midnight Mass.

At least she has her family and friends around - there will be a happy ending for all, won't there?

About the Author

P enelope lives on an island off the coast of Kent, England, with her four children and an elderly Jack Russell Terrier. A lover of murder mystery and cups of tea (served with a stack of digestive biscuits), she writes quaint cosy mysteries and other feel-good stories from a corner table in the vintage tea shop on the high street. Penelope loves nostalgia and all things retro. Her taste in music is also very last century.

Find out more about Penelope at www.penelopecress.com.

Want to know more?

Greenfield Press is the brainchild of bestselling author Steve Higgs. He specializes in writing fast paced adventurous mystery and urban fantasy with a humorous lilt. Having made his money publishing his own work, Steve went looking for a few 'special' aut

To find out more and to be the first to hear about new releases and what is coming next, you can join the Facebook group by copying the following link into your browser - www.facebook.com/GreenfieldPress.

Free Books and More

Want to see what else I have written? Go to my website.

https://stevehiggsbooks.com/

Or sign up to my newsletter where you will get sneak peeks, exclusive giveaways, behind the scenes content, and more. Plus, you'll be notified of Fan Pricing events when they occur and get exclusive offers from other authors because all UF writers are automatically friends.

Copy the link carefully into your web browser.

https://stevehiggsbooks.com/newsletter/

Prefer social media? Join my thriving Facebook community.

Want to join the inner circle where you can keep up to date with everything? This is a free group on Facebook where you can hang out with likeminded individuals and enjoy discussing my books. There is cake too (but only if you bring it).

https://www.facebook.com/groups/1151907108277718

Printed in Great Britain
by Amazon

36358274R00185